WILL

VERONIQUE KODJO

Ordering Information:

Prime Seven Media
518 Landmann St.
Tomah City, WI 54660

Printed in the United States of America

PART 1

SF (Safe Space): Profile Presentation of William, 22 Years Old

I'm a bit of a peculiar person; I can't really have breakfast in the morning because I'm not hungry and especially because I don't feel well doing it. I know, the most important meal of the day, etc., but I'm not interested. However, if I wake up late or wait until 11 a.m., I might feel a slight hunger, and I can only eat savory foods at that time, like rice; I love it, just like my mother. Not Asian, I promise, more of a mixed race.

Then, I absolutely cannot eat anything sweet in the morning or drink water on an empty stomach, or I will vomit in either case. Yet, I can promise my stomach is not fragile at all. Anyway, you can already understand that I am "high maintenance."

Finally, I come from a very large family, especially on my mother's side, middle-class and very religious, Catholic Christian. It's clear that they are very traditional and conservative. So, there aren't many subjects that can be discussed at family dinners, but a few are accepted. One good thing related to traditionalism is that it's something that unites us all, and I know I can count on everyone for almost anything, which makes us a very close-knit family that helps each other a lot.

Nevertheless, I am unfortunately afflicted by one of the "ills" that are not accepted by my loving family. I am bisexual. I know I said "ill," and it's cliché not to accept oneself and even to deny one's sexuality and consider it unnatural, a sin, and to deceive oneself, bla bla bla i get it hold your horses. I've already said that I don't care about your opinion and that I just want to be heard. So, be quiet. I was saying that I struggle to embrace my sexuality and that it's hard to silence a part of myself.

So, reconcile everything I've just told you with the fact that I am hypersensitive, very empathetic, and have a horrible complex that forces me to do everything to be loved by everyone. Not to mention that my empathy comes with an incredible ability to adapt based on where I am and who i am with. In summary, this makes me a very sensitive person who always feels too much while completely hiding everything he feels and changes his personality depending on the group of people around him to the point of not knowing what his true personality is anymore. Let's say I gave myself a multiple personality disorder on purpose and it is biting me in the arse, i don't know which is the real one if any. It's true that I can say I am very close to my parents and my brother, sister, and my best friend. Yet, even with them, even if I say what I really think, I still can't access my true personality. Because, I don't know what it is since I've forgotten it a long time ago, and especially, there are still things that I can't tell them. By the way, none of them knows that I'm bi because for me, saying it is accepting it, while at the moment, I refuse to do so. I am very heterosexual, and that's it. I am not homophobic I promise and anyway i don't Care what you all think. Again.

Understand me, I have nothing against being bisexual, but I just know that I didn't want to have to hide a part of my life from my mother or break her heart by telling her everything. So, I thought blocking a part of my personality for everyone to be happy was 'here is the stupid urge to always please others.' Conclusion: the best choice in my eyes is to be what I am not. You'll see that it's not really a conclusive life philosophy—if you're at all intelligent, you already know that.

You must have noticed that I didn't describe myself—I just said I was mixed race; more precisely, my mother is of Togolese origin, and my father is French. So I have very curly hair and hazel eyes, and I am quite fit since I love sports, especially swimming. I'm exactly 1.75m tall. I won't describe myself further feeling creepy so you can imagine me however you want; I always find descriptions tedious anyway. And I won't describe the other people I'm going to talk about either; I'll just mention their general appearance—hair age, height—and say that relatively, I find them hot or not if I feel like it. You've got the idea; I'm really bad at descriptions. This way you can, I don't know, imagine the people however you want based on their characters; I find that much more interesting, far more conclusive, and maybe even better for your imagination.

So, here we are. Other than my life philosophy, I see myself as quite handsome, lol. Yes, I still have some self esteem if talking about physique. I don't live alone; I live in an apartment in Paris with my best friend, Ray, who is studying management at a business school as a young heir from a rich family—you see what I mean, right? While I study architecture. I won't burden you with my courses and what they're about; I just want you to have an idea of the kind of things I love. So, I love drawing, I love buildings, the beauty of things, creating, as Ray says. Just because of a little discussion we had together the summer before our final year. I think I should tell the story. It is actually kind of funny.

<u>**Comment Section**</u>

Monday, 9 PM

WdoBest_84_ : Hi, I'm Laura. I saw your profile, and I thought you would be really interesting to study?

Seetrought93 : To study? I thought the app was just about chatting and opening up without judgment. "WITHOUT JUDGMENT" and there you go, so I don't find the word "study" very appropriate in that spirit.

WdoBest_84_ : I just wanted to say that, you seem like a lot I am going to have fun with you.

Seetrought93 :I'm not sure I feel safe with you.

WdoBest_84_ : Really ? I'm sure that after reading your profile, no one will want to talk to you.

Seetrought93 :Meh.

WdoBest_84_ : And I feel you're starting to enjoy my sassy side.

Seetrought93 :Maybe.

WdoBest_84_ : Well, there you go. So, what did you want to talk about with your long introduction to the profile?

Seetrought93 : About everything and nothing. Just really to say everything I think.

WdoBest_84_ : Okay.

Passeureby_102 : 🚶 Too much drama here 🚶

So, as I was saying at the beginning...

<u>**Comment Section**</u>

WdoBest_84_ : Little pause, I think you really misunderstand how this site works.

Seetrought93 : How so?

WdoBest_84_ : You can use as many aliases as you want and describe or not describe; it's your point of view, but you're not really here to write a novel but to discuss and receive advice from someone you don't know on subjects you can't discuss with friends or family. So, no need for a long introduction or anything; either we chat, or you act like you're having sessions with a daily confidant; it's up to you to decide if that still works for you.

Seetrought93 : Yes, of course. Well, can I just finish with my anecdote for today?

WdoBest_84_ : I hope it's fun.

Seetrought93 : It is from my point of view, so the only point of view that matters.

WdoBest_84_ : Meh.

Seetrought93 : You are really going to be annoying.

WdoBest_84_ : But you will love it.

Seetrought93 : Hum.

The-hot-girl_42 : Can you too stop flirting so he can continue ?

Passeureby_102 : 🚶 she is not wrong completely ! 🚶

WdoBest_84_ : Oh that is enough already.

So, here it goes...

I still remember that day as if it were yesterday. We were about to start our last year of high school, and Ray had come to pick me up so we could enjoy our last Saturday of vacation together. We decided to do some biking in the morning with Liam, and Antoine, two other childhood friends of ours, whom we would pick up afterward. I can't remember exactly what led to the discussion beside the fact that the next week we would officially be seniors, but we started talking about our future plans, and when we arrived at Liam's house, he was waiting for us at the door, and the discussion was quite lively.

- So, you're going to business school and take over your dad's company like the boring oldest child you are, right, Ray?
- After studying marketing and management.
- So boring and pedestrian;
- If you say so, but at least I know what I will be doing unlike someone i know ;
- What are you guys talking about?
- About Will's lack of organization regarding his future.
- Nothing new then.
- Exactly.
- Ugh! *I said while looking up, showing how annoyed i was.* Where's Antoine?
- Oh, he decided to join us later; he spent the whole night talking to the girl he met at Sebastian's party. Lucky him. And poor girl he is so boring sometimes.
- I see, he needs to catch up on sleep. And he is not boring he us just peculiar and passionate.
- Exactly. Yeah right not boring at all.
- So, what are you going to do. *Ray asked Liam coming back again to the subject of our future.*
- Gogo dancer seems like a job at my level.
- You're stupid! Like so Dumb it gives headaches.
- Okay, more seriously, are you really going to enter senior year not knowing where you'll go?
- I'll probably follow you wherever you go, Ray.
- No thanks, I'm tired of you. *He sais smirking.*
- Well, actually, I found something that interested me, but I'm not sure if it's a good idea.
- What is it? Knowing you, we're not expecting anything impressive.
- I'm going to get rid of you in a really violent way, Liam. A grusome death is awating you.

– Come on, just tell us. *Ray said, seeming impatient to hear the next absurdity I was going to share.*

– Okay! Actually, I did a little research, and there's a job as an interior architect designing objects for decoration and everyday life that would be ecological.

– Oh, I see, interesting;

– Yes, but I don't just want to work inside; I want to be a dual architect if that makes sense, both exterior and interior. I want to create things to put in houses I would design myself.

– Oh, you want to create things! *They both said in unison.*

– No, but really, you're bastards; I don't even know why I bother talking to you.

– It's fine. But joke aside, I think it's a good idea. Even though I feel you have your work cut out for you.

– You think so, Ray? Honestly, I wonder if I should just focus on writing and pursue literary studies.

– Well, those are two diametrically opposed projects.

– Yes, you see why I'm telling you I don't know what I'm going to do?

– Hmm, I understand better. But still almost not the time to be debating anymore.

– Well, let's not worry about it now. It's better to focus on biking today, and we'll see the rest later.

– You're totally right. Are you ready to go Liam?

– Yep, let's go.

<u>Comment Section</u>

Seetrought93 :And that's how I ended up with this little 'inside joke' about people who create. Fun, huh?

WdoBest_84_ : Meh.

Seetrought93 : Is that the instend of your vocabulary ?

WdoBest_84_ : When I'm bored, yes.

Seetrought93 : 😳 gosh.

Joker-99- : Got to admit it is kind of lame.

Seetrought93 : You just have no taste.

Anyway, there you go! We live in an apartment with three bedrooms and a living room, Ray and I. The bedrooms are relatively average, not too big and not too small; we have a living room directly adjacent to the open kitchen, a small dining area next to it. Our rooms are separated by a single wall, so it's pretty easy to hear each other when one is occupied, if you know what I mean, and the third room is relatively close to the front door, right next to the shared bathroom, which is linked directly to the toilets. Anyway, a brief tour of the apartment. I met Ray in sixth grade; he's someone I've always gotten along with, one of the closest people to me. Personally, I find him quite attractive; he has red hair and green-gray eyes. He's 1.95m tall and pretty muscular—a true heartthrob. That's what I'd say about his appearance. So we get along really well; we've always been close, so it was a given for us to live together and come to Paris for our studies. For now, I wouldn't say I complain. He's not much of a party person, and it's rare for him to come home late at night; he usually stays with his cousins, whom he hangs out with most of the time, or he comes home pretty early. So, he's easy to live with, not complicated, enjoys preparing meals, and I love that because I do too and he actually cooks really well. Sometimes we argue about who makes dinner; we do it together and argue while doing it, about who is in charge, who gives orders, that kind of stuff, but generally, everything goes well. We like the same things, we get along great, and my mom loves him; in fact, I have the impression that he is more her son than I am because she asks about him more than she does me, but that's another story. The only thing we never agree on is maybe my frivolous pursuits, my romantic escapades, my many girlfriends who never last long, for a reason I'll explain later.

<u>Comment Section</u>

WdoBest_84_ : Ooooh hot guy alert can you present him to me. I wouldn't mind hitting that. And he cooks too, total package.

Joker-99 : I'am in too if he prefers.

Seetrought93 : Seriously Now you are invested, interested ?

WdoBest_84_ : Yeah and it seems you are too seeing how you described him.

The-hot-girl_42 : You got to admit you described him like a hotty.

Seetrought93 : Not really i am just objectif i don't at all see him like that.

WdoBest_84_ : If you say so.

Seetrought93 : Hum.

The reason I'm here is to find out—or rather rediscover—who I really am. Finally, why my life has become what it is. Right now, I'm seeing a girl; in fact, it happens very rarely for me to be single. I'd say it's because I don't really like to be alone, or i am addicted to sex maybe, no just the alone thing anyway ; I've always been the romantic type, so I've always wanted to be someone interesting enough to have people around me, and I don't know, build something as beautiful as what my parents have, but I find that it doesn't suit me very well. In fact, I feel that because I'm very interested in what surrounds me and very curious, I often want change and hate being bored. I don't know, having something happening in my life is very important because I'm the type to lose interest in someone much faster than I got interested in them. I love the kind of relationship that allows me to feel alive, so being very honest by nature, when I'm bored, I abandon, and I say it almost immediately. This has given me a very bad reputation that I don't think I deserve. I mean am I not allowed to get bored ? At least I don't lie and cheat. So there you have it. That happens to me often. I get interested and then abandon. But don't hold that against me from the start; it's not my fault; it's just that when I reach out to someone, it's because they intrigued me and when the novelty or rather the mystery is gone, so am i. It's what often happens, I'd even say always, but I don't want to sound pretentious; I connect fairly easily, and I make a friend, or more often, I date, and it starts all over again.

<u>Comment Section</u>

WdoBest_84_ : I think you've gotten lost in your monologue again.

Seetrought93 : Yes, but I think it's super interesting. Writing helps one know oneself. I find more and more things to say to ensure you get to know me properly and give me good advice, I suppose.

WdoBest_84_ : Well, if you insist, tomorrow I want a summary of the day; we'll gradually find your true personality in all this clutter just by observing your reactions, I guess.

Seetrought93 : Okay.

WdoBest_84_ : Quick question: do you have a little crush on your friend Ray?

Seetrought93 : Nope, he's a great buddy but, his love life is kind of weird. Not really my type. Like I said so move on ?

WdoBest_84_ : Meh, from what I understand, you're the same, i mean you have a weird relationship habit so I don't see why all the judgment.

Seetrought93 : Nope, not at all; I'm going to explain everything much more clearly.

WdoBest_84_ : Okay. I am sorry i offended you, you weirdo. Please don't make me go through another monologue.

Seetrought93 : You are such pain.

WdoBest_84_ : Thank you.

Passeureby_102 : 🚶 Sill boring around here. 🚶

Seetrought93 : what is the problem with tha guy anyway.

So, as I was saying, it goes like this:

First, I meet someone who seems interesting or intriguing to me, so I approach and start a conversation, and generally, it ends with exchanging contact information and that's how it starts. I know, it's like I'm describing myself going grocery shopping, but oh well.

Then I find myself in a relationship that at the beginning excites me a lot, but then it becomes increasingly tedious because, frankly, who can really see their partner every day and all the time non-stop without it becoming repetitive and tiring? Anyway, at some point, I'm bound to get fed up and want to stop. It's completely normal.

As I begin to understand, now that I'm writing it down, I feel like people like to be glued to each other, so there must be something kind of wrong with me.Oh well who cares i am right. However, I should clarify that at one point in my life, when I was in my first or second year, I started researching my sexuality because we don't grow up in this time of our lives without searching a bit, and I realized in a certain way that I'm a demisexual person. I don't know if it's very well-known, but it's a person who needs to know people intimately; that is to say, to be friends, to be interested, to have a certain connection with that person before being romantically interested in them. So indeed, for that person, but the more we talk, the more we're interested in each other, the greater the chances that I'll feel a real sexual attraction or not. And as soon as it happens, I feel like I have to try hard or rather I feel this crazy urge to get completely into it, to go all in and everything. But going all in for me maybe isn't going all in for everyone. For me, going all in means "yes, let's go out and all that," but it never means "let's go out together and see each other 24/7, come spend weeks at my place." I'm someone who is very homebody and very closed off, so I don't know, I need to find myself alone, maybe once in a while. Now that I think about it, maybe the fact of always wanting to please, of always wanting to be liked, of constantly changing personality around people, thinking about how not to hurt people makes me just tired of being with people, and therefore I may often want to withdraw, to be alone, and to search for myself, that's all. Because technically, when I don't feel well, I'd rather have happy people around, preferably go out dancing, blow off some steam, you know what I mean? But with a lot of people, not really just one person who sticks to me like a sticker. I find that annoying. I'm already learning a lot just from this little introduction.

Comment Section

WdoBest_84_ : I see you're the kind of person who is always thinking deeply about everything until loosing your mind over it. A proper overthinker.

Passeureby_102 : 🚶 Yeah an annoying person. 🚶

Seetrought93 : Yeah, a little, but isn't that a good thing? Look at all the conclusions I've come to just by writing and thinking at the same time.

WdoBest_84_ : Lame. Well, that's not how it works! You need to give yourself a bit more time, but especially, you need to take the time to listen to the person you're talking to, that is to be precise, me, in the now and then.

Seetrought93 : Yes, I'll try.

WdoBest_84_ : I see you're not really boyfriend material.

Seetrought93 : Of course I am, I'm great! You just need to not turn into a sticker.

WdoBest_84_ : Meh. People tend to want to spend time with their boyfriends or girlfriends, but you don't really want to do that often. Isn't that a bit discouraging?

Seetrought93 : Hum. C'est bon passons à autre chose.

WdoBest_84_ : Do you think I can't speak French? We are not moving on until you agree with me or convince me.

Seetrought93 : Fine. You're right.

WdoBest_84_ : Good. So you came to this app just to spill your fuckboy stories. That might be interesting to observe; I haven't really had the chance to see exactly how this specimen of guy operates.

Seetrought93 : I am not a fuckboy.

WdoBest_84_ : Typical response.

Seetrought93 : No, but I'm serious; I'm not one.

WdoBest_84_ : I'm joking, don't worry. I mean half joking to be precise.

Seetrought93 : Ugh.

WdoBest_84_ : You are so easy to rattle.

Seetrought93 : You're not funny.

WdoBest_84_ : Well, then tell me about your day. We can keep it simple, but after that you can write "Monday entry" or "Thursday entry"... and there you go. You tell whatever you want whenever you want. Like in a blog or whatever.

Seetrought93 : Good idea I suppose.

WdoBest_84_ : And please quit writing long sentences.

Passeureby_102 : 🧍 She is kind of right. 🧍

Seetrought93 : Fine 😳

WdoBest_84_ : Okay, perfect then.

I get out of bed like every Saturday morning...

<u>Comment Section</u>

WdoBest_84_ : Another beginning of your monologue?

Seetrought93 : You're really annoying, you know that?

WdoBest_84_ : No.

Seetrought93 : Hum, but let me talk finally. Shut up. I'll pretend our conversation is like journal entries or a wonderful book about my thrilling life, and I would appreciate it if the journal commentary was less annoying. No one likes sassy diaries. Also stop interrupting me go do something else while i am writing and come back later.

WdoBest_84_ : No and also I think your life is precisely the opposite of thrilling. But you know what, write however you want; I'm here to look for ideas for my novels, so I suppose you're making things a bit easier for me by writing like that.

Seetrought93 : I forbid you to use my life's narrative. I know it's exciting, but that's not a reason.

WdoBest_84_ : I don't even want to use it. I feel like you're the ultimate cliché of a lost fuckboy, and that would bore my readers. I'd prefer to be inspired by all the ideas I can get to make it more interesting and original.

Seetrought93 : I hate you.

WdoBest_84_ : Meh. Shall we continue with your boring Saturday ?

Seetrought93 : I'll keep going because I want to, not because you asked me to.

WdoBest_84_ : Yeah yeah.

Seetrought93 : Hum. I had completely forgotten an important detail; thanks for making me angry, which made me remember it immediately. So as I was saying...

I opened my eyes and immediately regretted it because I hadn't closed the curtains of the window that is directly in front of my bed, and the sun had decided to be the first to say good morning to me this Saturday morning. What a great idea to sleep with the curtains pulled; what an idiot. I took a look at my phone, which was next to me, despite my mother's efforts to make me lose this habit. 8:55 AM. Not bad. I rubbed my eyes and got out of bed.

Like every Saturday morning I changed and headed to the gym to get on the treadmill in the gym in the basement of our building. But before going down, I noticed my phone ringing. It was my mom.

- Hello, Mom.
- Hey, darling, how are you?
- Good, and you?
- Good, I just finished my workout, I'm going to turn the music up loud in the living room to make sure I wake your brother and sister.
- But it's only 9 AM, and it's Saturday.
- We don't care. Your dad and I are wide awake, right? You too, by the way, so it's time. We're going to do some cleaning today, so it's better to start early, and all that with music.
- Yes, you're right, all that with music.
- Anyway, it's not like you make less noise when you're at home. You're the one who started cranking up the music every Saturday; I'm just continuing your tradition.
- Hum.
- By the way, how's Ray doing?

At that moment, I noticed that the door to his room was open. He had probably gone to the bathroom.

- He just came out of his room.
- I hope you didn't wake him up by making a lot of noise.
- No, but you really become another person when it comes to Ray. Were you not just going to do just that to your childrens ? You blast music in your own children's ears to wake them up, but for Ray, he needs his beauty sleep?
- Exactly.

At that moment, Ray came out of the bathroom stretching noisily, bare-chested, showing off his abs with his V-line visible because his shorts were pulled low.

- Come on, are you going to dress decently and make less disgusting noise? You don't live alone, I remind you.

He completely ignores me and comes toward me, takes the phone from my hands to put it on speaker and places it on top of the refrigerator, all with a smug smile on his face.

- Hello, Aunt Marie, how are you?
- I'm good, my darling. I hope your brother isn't bothering you too much over there and that he's behaving. Sorry if he woke you up; it's probably because he doesn't know how to talk without shouting on the phone.
- *Ray's smile grows larger* .Don't worry, Aunt, I'm used to it. I deal with largerhim just fine; he's my LITTLE brother afterward. *He emphasizes the adjective "little."*
- I'm still here, you know? And out of the two of us, the most impossible to live with is you. And, for the umpteenth time, you're only three months older than me.
- I forbid you to speak like that to your older brother.
- Mom, I'm your eldest son; I don't have an older brother.
- I forbid you to speak so hurtfully in front of me.
- Yes, you're really being hurtful, LITTLE brother. *At this point he was grinning showing his entire set of ugly teeth.*
- Are you going to stop this already?

Ray is completely laughing now, that backstabbing jerk.

- Well, I'm going to do my workout, Mom. Big hugs, I'll call you back later, bye.
- Are you giving up?

- Shut up.
- Well, I'll leave you two then. I'll make sure your brothers are awake.
- Okay, hugs, love you, Mom.
- Big hugs, Aunt.

Hearing that, I rolled my eyes. What a brown-noser.

- Goodbye, my darlings.

And she hung up without giving us a chance to reply to anything. As usual, she is always in a hurry to hang up.

- Well, I'm heading down.
- Don't tire yourself out too much, LITTLE brother; I'll come down to join you in a few minutes."

I gave him a lovely middle finger before opening the door to exit under his hyena-like snickering.

Comment Section

WdoBest_84_ : You seem to have a very good relationship with each other.

Seetrought93 : Yeah, I know, even though he's sometimes a big jerk; he's not a bad friend.

Passeureby_102 : 🚶 **contradicion here !** 🚶

WdoBest_84_ : You, Shut it !

Joker-99- : Whaou violent !

WdoBest_84_ : Hum.

Seetrought93 : What, do you have something to add?

WdoBest_84_ : Have you ever had a crush on him?

Seetrought93 : No God what is your issue with our friendship being just that ? As far back as I can remember, I've always seen him as one of my best friends, if not my best friend. But he's too much of a player for me. Plus, he's never had a serious relationship with any guy that I know of.

WdoBest_84_ : So you've thought about it a bit. It just for my book you guys would make a good couple like in that BL i once watched called HIStory 4. I just want to know how to speen a best friend's love Story in a very realistic way.

Seetrought93 : Don't use me for your book. And no, well, I did wonder about it at one point because someone asked me the same thing. Physically yeah, I'm not blind, but really not my type, fuckboys. And it would feel weird. Besides, I don't date guys, remember ?

WdoBest_84_ : Yes, and you prefer to be the fuckboy of the couple.

Seetrought93 : I'm sick of you. Otherwise, yeah, that's not my type at all.

WdoBest_84_ : Meh.

Seetrought93 : I'm serious.

WdoBest_84_ : Okay, if you say so. But I'm quite intrigued. It's weird that as a bisexual and demisexual person, you've never had the urge to get under his pants. He really sounds hot.

Seetrought93 : Nope, never. I've had crushes on other guys but never on him.

WdoBest_84_ : Is he super ugly? And your description skills are really bad?

Seetrought93 : No, I told you he's super hot. If you saw the kind of people he brings home?

WdoBest_84_ : I imagine it's another fuckboy.

Seetrought93 : I don't know. No one has ever complained. I guess he's pretty honest.

WdoBest_84_ : Okay, fine.

Seetrought93 : Well, back to my day's events?

WdoBest_84_ : Fine, go ahead.

Seetrought93 : Anyway, the rest of the morning and afternoon wasn't very interesting. It was filled with meals, naps and all that. Typical lazy Saturday. Nothing particularly special; but in the evening we had planned to see my friends, so let me tell you about the evening so you have a little idea of who they all are.

WdoBest_84_ : Okey, dokey.

We agreed to meet at a bar around Châtelet in the first arrondissement for a drink, and then we'll go wherever the night takes us.

Around 9 PM, we were all there. I'm going to do the introductions; we're at a round table, so I'll start with my left. Right next to me was Ray, who you already know and who was drinking a martini. Then, Liam and Antoine, both with a guiness in hand. They are childhood friends who I've known for a long time; I must have been two or three years old when I met them. After that, there's André and Hannah, whom Liam and I met at a party one day when we had been abandoned by the others. Finally, just to my right, Alina, a girl I met during my first year of high school, and with whom I got along really well, and who became a close friend.

So how's this new year going so far for everyone? Started Antoine with a little smile on his face. I am sure he is excited as usual to start courses. Such a weirdo.

You have a talent for ruining the mood, don't you, Antoine? I said, rolling my eyes.

- Well, we need to start with serious topics before getting into debauchery so that's done, right Liam? *Ray responded, all smiles.*
- Yes, absolutely.
- So? Since you both agree, how's your studies going? Ray, Liam, or even you, Antoine?
- I'm a bit bored for now; I can't wait for the real stuff to start, as they say. *Responded Ray matter of factly.*

- Only you can be in the middle of your first semester and not find the year stifling in terms of workload. In a master's program, no less.
- Well, I'm not overwhelmed for now, either ? I think it started pretty well for now, *added Antoine.*
- I'm dead with my double master's, and I swear I don't even know where to turn my attention. *I said taking a big sip of my cocktail.*
- Yes, he's constantly complaining and working late; he's really hard to live with.
- I am swamped with work, thank you very much, asshole.
- Okay, now I don't have the right to speak my mind anymore?
- Is the little couple done?
- Yes, I think my wife is just on her period, when everything is annoying for no reason.
- Real girls present, Ray. So calm down.
- Sorry, Alina, so how's your year?
- Normal, nothing interesting, always stressful for normal people.
- Of course. So to sum up, Ray and Antoine are completely at ease. The rest of us are normal students, tired of it. Now we just have Hannah and André.
- Good summary, Liam. So me, I'm in between. I have work, but I like it a lot, especially the internship part.
- Good, Hannah, I'm a normal student who can't wait for it to be over, *sayed André.*
- Nope, normal student doesn't mean that, especially for people like Will; they love stress and fatigue. So he is very happy with his situation right now. Not looking forward to it to end.
- He is weird that way.
- Thanks, Ray, Alina, but I can express myself on my own thank you very much. Well, now I'd like to know how the debauchery part of the evening is going.
- Oh, I like how you think. Shots, everyone?
- Yes, Liam is treating us, so we should take advantage of it.
- I'm not treating; I'm proposing.
- Well, I'm coming with you, Liam. Anyone else volunteering?
- I'll join you.
- Thanks, Antoine, I'll bring you a guinnes, Will?
- Yep, thanks.
- And, can we ask for special orders, or do we need to be your wife to get special treatment?
- You should get up Hannah, we are just getting the shots.
- I see.

- Well, I'm going with them, so I can take special orders but I'm only taking orders accompanied by credit cards.
- Even me?
- Especially you, Alina, so I'll bring a ton of margaritas. said Liam.
- I want a sex on the beach.
- Okay, Hannah. Others?
- A whisky for me.
- Same.
- So, a guiness for Will, a sex on the beach for Hannah, a martini fo Ray i guess, two whiskies for Antoine and me, and margaritas for the rest. Now, where are the credit cards, and I'm also charging the shots.
- Stingy.
- And proud of it. Give me the cards.
- No need, Will; I can pay for you.
- So good to have a husband; I'm jealous.
- Well, I'm inviting you then Alina.
- Thank you, bae. So we're in a love triangle?
- Seems like it said Ray with a neutral face.
- We're in an open marriage, aren't we, Ray?
- Hum.

So Liam, Antoine, and Ray got up to go to the bar to take the orders.

- So, while we wait for them to come back, now that the work-study topic is closed, what do you say we go to the romance department?
- I recognize you well there, Hannah; always ready for a little gossip.
- As you say, Will, so you start because for you, it'll be quick and uninteresting.
- Oh, thanks a lot; that's nice.
- I don't think she's wrong, you know, dear. Your only lasting relationship is with Ray, and that's not a real one.
- It is a real one, thank you very much, Alina. Anyway, you are unfortunately right; I'm with nobody, so for today, it's short. I mean as of tomorrow i am single.
- Having a break up planned tomorrow.
- That's the plan
- Poor Girl
- I am inviting her to eat

- Of course you are. And it makes the heartbreak all better. Alina answered, rolling her eyes at me.
- But you sure have a side piece somewhere.
- Not at all. Just told you that I was busy.
- Never stopped you.
- Fine, your turn, Antoine. Save me from these two girls.
- Okay, but I can't entertain them for long because I'm not with anybody either.
- Another fuckboy.
- Yes, Antoine, how many slaps for the current school year?
- None, Hannah. I'm not subscribed to slaps; it happened just once this year, and since then, I can't breathe. I won't tell you anything anymore. And, I don't understand girls; I don't understand why it's so hard for them to understand that I'm not very good at long-term relationships; I say it almost every time, and I'm pretty honest about it.
- Maybe I should tell you what he told Liam and me.
- What did I do again?
- Nothing, dummy; we're discussing Antoine's breakup.
- Oh, okay, I see. No need to be so aggressive, you know, Alina.
- Hum.

Our three servers had come back, each with a tray in hand, and were struggling to place each drink in front of everyone.

- Interesting, what brought this discussion up all of a sudden?
- Oh, but you know, dear, just Hannah being very nosy as always.
- I see.
- Is the little couple done?
- I'd like to continue.

Ray and I looked at each other and smiled. Then I replied to Hannah with the same smile on my face.

- We're done, you can continue. I'm certain now that you're single and jealous; that's why I forgive you.
- He got you there.
- Shut up, André, and we all know I am not single. Well, so he came to join us for dinner the last time you stood us up Will, with his entire left cheek all red, hair messy, and his gaze lost in space, as usual.

- I wasn't there.
- No, you were sick; now shut up, André.
- She's going all in, it's scary.

She gave me a death glare upon hearing that and continued speaking while staring at me with that look for a little while.

- As I was saying, he looked like he had had the most traumatizing experience of his life, so naturally, we asked him what was wrong, and he simply told us that he had the bad idea of breaking up with his girlfriend face to face. He should have done it by email after blocking her, the jerk.
- It's true that knowing Antoine, she doesn't know that jerk's address.
- Thanks a lot, Liam.
- No problem, bro.
- So, Liam asked him, but what did you do to get slapped like that? So he told us the biggest nonsense I've ever heard in my life. I assure you, it deserves an award.
- Tell us already and stop making it dramatic it is annoying?

There, she didn't just glare at me but gave me a punch after straightening up a bit to make sure to reach me. Completely violent.

- Ouch.
- Serves you right.
- You too, Alina?
- Okay, now shut up. Continue, Hannah.
- Thanks, Alina. So here's what he did. Deciding to break up, he asked her to meet him in the park where they often met, which just happened to be not very far from the restaurant where we were supposed to dine with him. Then when he saw her arriving, he kissed her and asked her to sit down, and then, just like that, he bluntly told her he wanted to break up, especially that he had to join us, so he couldn't stay with her for long.
- No, that's not true. I explained the reasons, namely that I didn't feel as involved as at the beginning, that I had sensed it for a while and thought it wasn't fair to continue when I felt nothing. And finally, I suggested staying with her for whatever time it would take because I could be late since I only saw you two, so it wasn't very important," he said, pointing at Liam and Hannah.

- Anyway, what she must have understood is what I said. Besides, being polite and caring while breaking up is illogical, but we always knew you were kind of insane so...
- The fact is, he never left any hints; keep in mind he was romantic and gentleman-like as usual, and then suddenly he tells her he hasn't been able to take it for a while. So she surprised him with a good slap.
- Exactly what he deserved.
- No, but I don't understand your point of view; would you have preferred he act like a jerk and especially that before the breakup, he treated her badly and distanced himself so that she could get a hint as you say?
- Well yes, maybe they could have found a solution if she'd noticed a change. And, above all, she wouldn't have been shocked like that. And then it's good to have some ammunition to complain about you afterward to feel better; otherwise, where's the point? This way, they don't feel like they lost much. Do you understand better, Will? Even if the best solution is to not break up at all
- Yes, I see; it's just so you can feel better about yourself. Ah, girls. The worst part is you seem to always find ammo to support your claims. So why even bother?
- Anyway, now we know what kind of jerk Antoine is. We expect nothing from him.
- Thanks a lot, Liam; that's nice.
- With pleasure. Now let's move on to me. I met a handsome guy last night, and I think this time he was the good one.
- Meh.
- I mean, this will last more than three months this time. You're not nice either, Antoine.
- Well, the next is Ray.
- Single.
- Basics. Always the same answers with you. How do you function, exactly?
- I have a lot of laziness in me.
- Is he just faithful or is there a problem?
- Come on, girls, we want to hear from you too. Hannah?
- Still with Ryan. Alina?
- Single.
- Oh no, what a bore. But we forgot André; tell us something better than single.
- Not in a relationship.
- Great, thanks, I said, rolling my eyes. Well, shall we make this shot? To being single?
- To being single, they all replied together.

The night continues like that with alcohol flowing as much as we can pay for and discussions ranging from the most serious to the silliest. I completely forgot that, in our current society, it's common to introduce people by their respective sexual inclinations, so I'll add a little note. I'm a guy, and I'm bisexual, Ray is a pansexual guy, Liam is a bisexual boy with polyamorous tendencies, Antoine is a cisgender boy very heterosexual, André is non-binary primarily attracted to women, and finally, Hannah is a very heterosexual girl. Oh, I forgot Alina, who is pansexual and is, even though I doubt it sometimes, a girl.

<u>Comment Section</u>

Seetrought93 : So there you go, my friends ! Then again, I have other friends at university, but no need to talk too much about them, right?

WdoBest_84_ : As you wish.

Seetrought93 : Yes, I'm a bit lazy.

WdoBest_84_ : So that was your night yesterday?

Seetrought93 : Yep, then there's this morning too.

WdoBest_84_ : Do you remember what I told you about the previous night's event? Well, I said it as a joke to my friends but today I really had a break up scheduled. So let me tell you about my morning. Then, dare to say my life isn't interesting.

Jerome666 : It is not.

Passeureby_102 : 🚶 Could not have said it better ! 🚶

I woke up very late the following Sunday because we drank lots, but mostly because I had a date with Sarah. We've been arguing 24/7 for weeks because apparently, I'm not attentive enough or care too little about her and everything that could happen to her. If she wants a gentleman, she can go see Antoine. Although she will regret it like all of his exes did. No, but it's not possible. It seems like I do everything wrong, even after a year. Or rather, after a year, I'm not moving forward enough or fast enough.

Anyway, I get up, have breakfast, take a shower, get dressed, and it's off to this last date. How funny I am; great right ? Anyway, when I pass by Ray's room to reach the door, he sees my funeral expression and says good luck. I'm sure he knows where I'm going and what I'm going to do. I don't know how, but he always knows.

I don't need to tell you that I take my time getting to the meeting point, but I manage to arrive eventually. And, she is already there, sitting at a table by the window. I walk hesitantly toward her, wearing a smile as wide as it is fake. I don't know if I should kiss her or greet her, and I debate while slowly walking towards her. Eventually, she responds for me as soon as she sees me coming, because she stands up and once I'm close enough, she kisses me unexpectedly. I respond hesitantly, and she surely realizes this since she stops very quickly.

- Hello!
- Hi. So, did you have fun with your friends yesterday?
- Yes, thank you.
- And, I suppose it was even better since I wasn't there.
- Stop, Sarah, don't start. I told you that no one came with their girlfriend or boyfriend; it was just with friends.
- I don't think they would have complained; you didn't want me to come.
- That's true.
- What?
- I didn't especially want you to come.
- You don't even hide it anymore.
- No, since it's precisely why I came to talk to you.
- I suppose so. I wanted to be sure of it, which is why I kissed you.
- So?
- I'm sure, I think we should stop this.
- I agree with you.
- Clearly, you didn't even pretend to hesitate.
- I'm not going to insult your intelligence by doing that.
- My intelligence, huh? Good reply.
- I'm sorry, Sarah.
- I suppose you really are.
- I am.
- Well, are you going to let me go? I ordered a good ribeye and I'd like to enjoy it alone.

I had just lifted my eyes to look directly into hers and noticed they were unusually wet. I didn't want to be there if she cried, especially since I felt it would only worsen things for both her and me. So I got up from the chair where I had sat, and I offered her my hand because I didn't know what else to do.

- Enjoy your meal.
- Thanks?

She gave me a sad smile and I returned it. And I left without looking back until I reached the nearest subway station. When I arrived back at the apartment and passed by Ray's room again, he tossed out:

- So you're really single now?
- Yep.
- And, wasn't it too hard?
- No. I got exactly what I deserved. It's her that it was too hard for.
- What a jerk!
- Thank you so much.
- With pleasure.
- I'm going to rest.
- Go ahead.

I told you he was aware, that jerk; and instead of helping me feel better, he mocks me. I'm going to bed instead and sleep all day, ignoring him. That should teach that jerk a lesson.

<u>**Comment Section**</u>

WdoBest_84_ : Is that what you call interesting? Just another one of your breakups based on the boredom you seem to feel every time things get serious, Mr. Fuckboy?

Passeureby_102 : 🚶 At least he is consistent. 🚶

Seetrought93 : Yeah, well, you're annoying me too; I'm going to go back to bed;

WdoBest_84_ : You're the annoying one. That's why Ray did not bother to Find out how you were he knows you don't care.

Seetrought93 : I do,come on! I am not a monster.

WdoBest_84_ : I am sure you feel more relieved than sad.

Seetrought93 : Well ...

WdoBest_84_ : Well.

Seetrought93 : It was not going well.

WdoBest_84_ : Hum.

Seetrought93 : I am tired bye.

WdoBest_84_ : Hum.

Seetrought93 : Ugh

_ One weeks later _

<u>**Comment section**</u>

Seetrought93 : Hey, I just saw that you logged in.

WdoBest_84_ : Hello, it's been a while. What have you been up to?

Seetrought93 : Nothing, uni, sleep, and repeat.

WdoBest_84_ : I knew you didn't have anything exciting in your life.

Seetrought93 : I was going to tell you about something fun that happened today.

WdoBest_84_ : Okay, go ahead, I'm listening.

Passeureby_102 : 🚶 reading 🚶

WdoBest_84_ : Shut it already.

Entry Saturday

Today, we had decided to go for a walk together, but laziness ultimately pushed us to stay in the apartment and watch a movie.

- Well, it's good we decided to watch a movie, but what do you specifically want to watch, Ray?
- You were the one who suggested it, so try to put in more effort.
- I suggest you choose.
- I see. You're really impossible to live with.
- You adore me; otherwise, you wouldn't be here after five years.
- Hum, maybe I'm a bit of a masochist.
- It is true
- I love you too.
- Meh.
- You know you don't always have to be dubious; we'll find something to watch okay ?
- I'll make popcorn in the meantime. Sweet for you and salty for me, okay?
- Hum, if you say so; I'll look at what options we have.
- Okay.

After checking my Netflix list and then his, which is surprisingly similar, I decided to put on a Christmas movie since it's the season and he hates that, but to be original "check out the sarcasm," I chose a gay one.

After a while, he comes back with two bowls and hands me one before sitting down on the couch right next to me to see what I had to offer. He gives me the middle finger upon seeing my choice, and I reply with a smile.

- You told me to choose, right?
- Yes, and I already regret it, but let's go.

In the end, we watch the movie, and Ray makes it a point to give insulting comments for each scene, which makes the film even funnier.

- Seriously, he can't just admit he's in love with his friend; he's gay too, so where's the problem? Keeping things like that to himself hurts, and it's extremely annoying. Guys, I swear.
- Until proven otherwise, you're one too, and by the way, are you talking from experience? Do you have a secret crush?
- Not at all.
- Are you sure?
- Yes, and by the way, you know your movie is trash; I'd rather take a nap. Just tell me when it's over.
- Come on, what's wrong with you all of a sudden?
- Nothing, just tired.
- Okay. But still, you can tell me if you have a little romantic problem; I'm here, I said with a smile.
- No thanks, *he says, giving me the middle finger.* You aren't the best person to talk to about that.
- Ouch, I'm hurt. That's not cool at all.
- I'm not lying.
- No, not really, I guess. But you don't have to say it; you're particularly mean tonight.
- Don't sulk, *he says, smiling widely and moving closer.*

He rested his head on my shoulder and smiled at me. I return his smile and start playing again. After a few minutes, he falls asleep on my lap, and I can feel his gentle breath on my lap, and I can't help but smile. He's too cute, but I better not tell him; he'll freak out and then annoy me to death. Anyway, I finish the movie, and I stay in front of my laptop's black screen until I fall asleep too. When I open my eyes again, Ray is in the kitchen cooking who-knows-what for dinner. I get up to offer him my

- So what are you making for us?
- Just rice with curry sauce.
- So you don't need help.
- Exactly.
- I'll clean up.
- Okay.

The rest of the evening, we dine and chat like we often do. A real married couple. I'm almost sure this will be the only serious relationship I'll ever have at this rate.

<u>Comment Section</u>

WdoBest_84_ : Is that what you call interesting ?

Seetrought93 : Yeah I was pulling your leg on purpose.

The-hot-girl_42 : You love repeating yourself don't you ? Stop flirting with him so he can continue.

WdoBest_84_ : You fick off, And beside Who says pulling your leg anymore ?

Seetrought93 : You know english is not my first language right ?

WdoBest_84_ : Not an excuse. I was going to ask why you write in English.

Seetrought93 : To have less french people read me and also i feel more detached writing in English rather than in french.

WdoBest_84_ : I see. You are Lucky I live in France too, for studies, or else I wouldn't be able to follow your crazy schedule.

Seetrought93 : I am not sure it is called being lucky you are a pain.

WdoBest_84_ : Yeah right. You love our talks.

WdoBest_84_ : Hum not denying it.

Seetrought93 : Shut It, I am leaving.

Jerom_666_ you guys are exhausting.

Entry Monday 5 AM.

Today, I found myself in this crazy dilemma, about Alina, whom I've known for a long time, since the end of middle school or rather the beginning of high school, and with whom I am really very close. It's true that from time to time, I've felt an interest in her, but it's rare for me to have friends that I can talk with as easily as I do with her. She's one of the few people, alongside Ray, Antoine and even Liam, with whom I talk with so much ease. So as she's a very close friend, a friend I don't want to lose, one of those rare people I can communicate with easily, I always put aside any interested may have. Recently, we've started flirting, and it's something that has started to freak me out because it means our relationship has changed, and given my track record regarding past relationships, we'll be together for anywhere from 3 months to a year and a half, which is really broad and not enough of a window. Like I said, a bad idea. There's a good chance it will end, and that's why I've made it a point to push her away and avoid anything that could happen between us. But lately, I feel a certain intent from her part to make things move along. I don't know if it's a good idea at all. It worries me, and that's why I'm bringing it up now because I don't want to lose a good friend just because I'm acting like a jerk, apparently. But I can tell you that until now I don't understand why I can be stigmatized for something like that because, in reality, we're all different, and we all react to our lives differently, and as a result, there's absolutely no chance that... Well, there's nothing that proves I'm doing anything on purpose, wanting to hurt or anything.

<u>Comment Section</u>

WdoBest_84_ : Come on you just said it yourself you can't stay With anybody more than three years, and i am sure it happened only once. You are not a good person so you don't want your friend to be hurt by a jerk like you. Good sentiment really.

Seetrought93 : You don't have to put it that way.

WdoBest_84_ : And what should I say.

Seetrought93 : That I am a good guy and since I am not sure I don't want to mislead her.

Passeureby_102 : 🚶 Delulu ! 🚶

WdoBest_84_ : Lie to yourself all you want.

Seetrought93 : Thank you bitch.

WdoBest_84_ : Pleasure.

Seetrought93 : Anyway, let me continue.

Jerome_666_ : Painfull conversation.

The-hot-girl_42 : to read right ?

Passeureby_102 : 🏃 Obvious police. 🏃

The-hot-girl_42 : Shut it already weirdo.

It's not always by telling myself, "yes, she's the one," that it really is. Because afterwards, I find myself bored, and the person hurt, and it's something I don't want to happen between Alina and me because she's someone I care about a lot and don't want to lose.

<u>**Comment Section**</u>

WdoBest_84_ : **Meaning you did not care about your other girlfriends ?**

Seetrought93 : **No it is not the say. Stop twisting my words.**

WdoBest_84_ : **Okay** 🤓

She is a friend with whom I talk a lot, by the way, we laugh a lot, we have our little nicknames, we have fun together, we have good conversations, we can go to the movies and chill together without it being awkward, we can talk for hours on the phone without getting annoyed ; she's, I don't know, a perfect friend, and that's it.

<u>**Comment Section**</u>

WdoBest_84_ : **Yeah and you are a perfect Dick.**

Seetrought93 : **Oh my god shut it already.**

WdoBest_84_ : **Fine.**

WdoBest_84_ : **But wait just a minute, what are you talking about? You can't come here writing as if you were in your journal without explaining what's going on because really, you can't start a story at the end.**

Seetrought93 : Yes, of course, I'll restart from the beginning; in fact, tonight about four hours ago, I was with my friend Alina.

WdoBest_84_ : Okay, I see, go on, I'm reading.

This Sunday, I had to meet up with Alina; Liam abandoned us and decided not to join us, and Antoine, who spends his time following Liam's moods, also decided not to come. So I find myself alone with her, nothing there that happened before and even if she was kind of wired with her allusions lately she is still the same person i guess.

Okay maybe I am lying to seeing I have a hard time telling myself that everything will go smoothly; and she's someone for whom I absolutely don't want to have the chance of being a jerk. So I felt a little nervous preparing to meet her. But I am decieded not to cancel on her feeling it woud be even wierder. The next day I dress casually, really simply, a t-shirt, pants, and sneakers, a wallet, a navigo, etc., in my pocket, all cool and everything.

We meet at a bar for drinks around 6 PM; we want to have a few drinks, eat some snacks, and chat among friends. There you go, simple no need to wory. When I arrive, she's already there, waiting for me, smiling, and waving her hand so I can see where she is, so I walk over smiling, we greet each other with a kiss on the cheek, and we sit down. As usual, we start chatting normally, like friends do. She asks me how I am; I tell her I'm doing well, that on Friday I had a library night, and it wore me out, that I rested a lot on Saturday, and that I finished my project that morning, and now I feel good, not too stressed. She tells me that on her side, things are going well, her studies are progressing, and she's working a lot on analytical computing, and she says it's interesting, that she has a lot of projects, that she's working hard, and that it's really exciting and all. Just that group projects bore her because it depends on how involved people are, so for her, it's quite tedious; she prefers working alone. In short, it's just formalities, we talk normally. She tells me that recently she was at her parents' for the weekend, that she saw her little brother who was learning to drive, and so they went for a drive together while he was driving, and at one point she says to me,

– You're not going to believe what that bastard did! I swear, you won't even believe it! Or you could never even imagine. Try to guess what that jerk pulled on me!

I then proceed to ask her what he did, and she replies,

- The jerk, I told him to drive to one of Boris's secret hideouts to grab a drink with his friends and have fun, you know. So I said, 'Drive, I'll take you there, and I'll show you where dad hides; that way, if he goes to hang out with them again. If Boris goes out again and says he's pissed off about some imaginary thing or that he's going to see his friends, you could tell mom and dad where they are, and they'll know.' So I decided to let him drive, to go forward, and we were on a winding road with turns; in short, not a straight road. As I was showing him the way, I told him to go straight, and the jerk, what does he do? He actually goes straight! When I was telling him to go straight, I was talking about following the road! But no, the guy understood, yeah, straight line. He ran off into the grass next to him and smashed the car like that! Against a tree, that jerk! It's ridiculous! The worst part is he saw the tree; he could have at least stopped, but no! Then I ask him, this idiot, why he did something like that, and why he left the road, and he replies that I didn't clearly say to follow the road, and that for him, going straight means that you have to go straight in a line, etc. And I thought to myself whogave me an idiot like for brother i swear i am cursed or something. He wrecked the car for nothing because he's really a turd. He really pissed me off this time, and I had to call a tow truck and say that I was driving. He was really dumb about it. The tow truck guy came, and I told him that yes, I was driving and that he hit me by mistake since that kid is an idiot, and that's why the car went into the tree. Fortunately, the guy understood, and we didn't have any problems. We sorted it all out, we made the report, and blah blah blah, but my brother wrecked the car like that, just like that! The big turd! No, but I swear that Antonin is really a big turd. It's ridiculous how much he exhausted me. It was funny afterward, but I'm never taking him in my car for anything ever again. But seriously, never! So I had to come by metro, which really irks me, but I have to admit it's a super funny anecdote when you forget that my car is unusable for now. In any case, there's no way I'm letting that kid borrow my car again, ever. Never! I don't want to deal with the metro because of him; it's absolutely horrible.
- Yeah, we all know that you're a rich, stuck up girl. Obviously you can't feel superior while driving alone in your car, feeling above all the other like your polluter friends if you don't have your car.
- Shut up already. I don't feel better than anyone; I just know how to drive. And I actully am better than you.
- Hum

- Why ? I'm usually fine and then like that, when at the end of the night you all end up having to deal with an Uber that costs who knows how much to get back, I can safely return home.
- While being drunk?
- Uh, not while being drunk, okay. Come on, most of the time, I'm the one supervising; I know you know that too, so shut up.
- Okay, fine.
- So there you go. *She sticks her tongue out at me and smiles.* By the way, seriously. Did Antoine and Liam abandon us without a second thought?
- You mean Liam abandoned us, and Antoine is following him?
- Yeah, exactly. What's with that?
- Not seeing his friends after a week. After he messed up my Friday by drinking shot after shot after shot, that jerk. I had to bring them back to my place for them to crash, and here's how I'm thanked. I'm definitely going to smash his head when I see him.
- Yeah, I know; that guy really isn't possible. How many people is he seeing right now?
- From what I remember, he's got two idiots; he's dating a girl and a weird guy he met in some bar, I don't know when. Anyway, a ridiculous polyamorous relationship. Not that I'm against polyamory, but I'm against him. He says it's the first time he's trying it, and he really likes it, and that's why he abanfonned us like he did. But yes, he's annoying as always!
- Just like always, Liam isn't someone we can count on, so we'll manage without him tonight.
- Yes, without him. No choice.
- So, everything good with studies and all?
- Well, aside from the little stress, I'm doing pretty well. I haven't started thinking about pills for suicide yet. So I guess I'm doing "quite a bit" well; let's just say I don't have any deep murder urges, or whatever.
- Okay, cool. So regarding relationships, love, and blah blah blah, how's that going? Still as disastrous as usual or what?
- Always. The girl I was dating, I broke up with her last Saturday for I don't know what reason. Oh yes, I remember; it was because she started asking me if she could come stay with me for three weeks because she missed me or some weird stuff like that. In short, the definition of the clingy, annoying girl to death.
- And there you go, again a story of deep boredom.
- Yeah, yeah. Same story.

- So as usual, I'm single.
- No you mean as usual, you're being your stupid self. Also that strangely you are single today but, by tomorrow morning, you'll have a date, right? You're going to meet a victimize before we go back, aren't you? It is your modus operandis right ?
- Absolutely not. I don't behave like that at all. It doesn't happen to me at all. Okay? I don't have a problem.
- Okay. Yeah, you absolutely don't have a problem when it comes to relationships with other human beings, do you?
- That's clear.
- Yes, that's it. Exactly, it's clear.
- So that means you're free and easy.
- Yeah, and you?

<u>Comment Section</u>

WdoBest_84_ : So your friend Liam is interested in polyamorous relashion ships. Interesting can i talk to him insted ?

Seetrought93 : No why ?

WdoBest_84_ : Well he seems to be more interesting to talk to than you

Seetrought93 : Fuck you.

WdoBest_84_ : I love you too.

Seetrought93 : You are such a pain.

WdoBest_84_ : And am really proud.

Seetrought93 : Hum. I am ending my story.

WdoBest_84_ : The boring One right.

Seetrought93 : 😳

So at that moment, I felt it was a very bad idea to ask that, but I had already asked, so there you go; I was waiting for the answer, and she told me no, she didn't have anyone, with a big smile. I noticed her hand getting closer to mine. I tried to slightly and imperceptibly move back so she wouldn't see and wouldn't feel sensitive about it. My glass was really close to my hand. I couldn't go too far without awakening a violent sense of rejection on her part, which I didn't want. So there you go; I stayed frozen there, and without warning, without understanding anything, she moved closer again, but this time not just her hand, and kissed me. In the moment, I was a bit shocked, so I responded, and then pushed her back slightly and looked at her questioningly, and she replied with something that left me completely stunned. She said that every time we do the same thing; we chat, flirt a little, I end up dating a bimbo who pops up from who knows where a few weeks later.

- So uh, I think this time I'm not going to pretend to lightly flirt and forget that end up continuing with your big nonsense; I'm just going to jump on you from the start, if that's it, right? In fact I don't if your like it. She added.
- That's it, it's done.
- Uh, I'm not really following you clearly at this precise moment.
- I think I was very clear. It's, hum, enough. I'm fed up with us not doing anything or just flirting without reason, beating around the bush, etc. I want us to go for it, whatever IT is. I'm asking you this simple thing "Give me a chance," don't answer right away. Think about it all night. Tell me, do we try, and get together and see how it goes? By the way, you responded to my kiss, so it wasn't bad, was it?

I put this awkward smile on my face. Without answering to her.

- So, I was wondering how it could have escalated so quickly; we were talking well for the last two hours, and there you go.
- So, did you plan this from the start?
- *She replied without any shame:*Yeah, and that's why I asked Liam not to come.
- Oh, you asked him not to come. So I dissed him for nothing. And you didn't say anything. Because, well, you thought it was funny, right?
- Yeah, I thought it was funny. You know me; I love playing with people,
- Damn. I suppose yeah, on that point, I know you. Anyway, let's head home.
- Already?
- Yes, well, Madam pulled out her big speech about not rushing. Think about it; don't reject me right away, so I'll just make life interesting for you and let you hang in there since you decided to pull one on me.

- Yeah, well, if it ends up like it's supposed to, I'm good with waiting a little night, but tomorrow morning at the first hour; otherwise, you're dead.
- Cool, well. We'll see if it's really good news or not.

She punches me on the shoulder.

- OK, okay. So, shall we go? You must need to take the metro, right? No need for you to walk me to the metro because I feel like I'm going to blush to my ears and you won't know how to react and it will end the night badly. So it's a lot better if I go back on my own. I've drunk a lot of alcohol, but I'm aware and awake now, considering the circumstances. I should have fled after the kiss if I followed logic, but I haven't done that, so it's better I go my own way now at least.
- I tink that an Uber would be fine; do you want one?
- No. thank you want me to wait with you.
- I just told you that I am about to blush so no go already.
- Yes, of course. Damn, *I think. I admit just a little;* I'm not quite in my right mind now.
- That's clear; I'm not too well either.
- Yeah, I see that.
- Well, bye.
- Bye

And we parted at the door, me to the left and she to the right. I have to admit I preferred the opposite because I had a huge detour to make so I wouldn't run into her at the metro station; great. But well, the simplest thing was not to complain and just go along with it. There you go.

When I got home, I was nothing but a big ball of thoughts, and I can say that's not very nice to see. On the train, I thought a lot, so my state was understandable. I looked like I was in a trance. I undressed while trying my best not to disturb Ray, even though I'm sure he wasn't sleeping, and I went to shower, all while staying lost in my thoughts; I think if someone had spoken to me at that moment, I would have clearly heard them, but I wouldn't have had the ability to respond; I really couldn't focus my thoughts on but one task, which was, find a way to get out of this mess. So, it was a shock for mz when fell asleep the moment my head finally met the pillow. I tought I was going to stay awake all night but it was not the case. Wiered, anyway Iwas clearly exhausted so I fell asleep and it was lucky because i had class at 8:30 AM to day.

<u>**Comment Section**</u>

Seetrought93 : Then I woke up, at 5 AM to write to you, did not sleep that long.

WdoBest_84_ : By the way, you didn't ask me what woke ME up?

Seetrought93 : I don't care; I'm too worried for now.

WdoBest_84_ : Seriously, what a jerk.

Seetrought93 : Fine. Why are you up?

WdoBest_84_ : Because my best friend just showed up in the middle of the night because he has problems with his sex friend.

WdoBest_84_ : Seriously ! Who has problems with a sex friend? That's not what that's for.

Seetrought93 : Enough about you.

WdoBest_84_ : Jerk.

Seetrought93 : Well, okay, I'm joking. Your friend is putting too much thought into a sex friend.

WdoBest_84_ : My thoughts exactly, but he refuses to understand that.

Seetrought93 : He's in love.

WdoBest_84_ : He's dumb.

Seetrought93 : What a loser Hum ? How does he manage to put up with you, and what made him think you could help him feel better, Miss Robot?

WdoBest_84_ : Shut up; he's doing just fine with me, I promise, especially considering how he spends his time whining.

Seetrought93 : Like I said, you're useless.

WdoBest_84_ : Well, continue your story; what are you going to do tomorrow?

Seetrought93 : I don't know; I wanted your opinion. You see, I was right; you're not very good at understanding and helping.

WdoBest_84_ : I think you still haven't understood that I don't want to help but find material for my writings.

Seetrought93 : Yeah, I know, but put in a little effort.

WdoBest_84_ : Not really in the mood. You write; I take the time to read; that's enough, thank you very much. By the way, your girl seems boring; don't date her.

Seetrought93 : I think you're right. Not about her being boring, but rather about the fact that it's best to refuse if I'm not sure at all.

WdoBest_84_ : If you want.

Seetrought93 : But how do I tell her?

WdoBest_84_ : That is a you problem does not concern me. You'll tell me tomorrow; I'm interested with what you will come up with.

Seetrought93 : You're really no help.

WdoBest_84_ : Exactly. Way to point out the obvious. Good night until tomorrow I mean latter today

Passeureby_102 : 🚶 Obvious police ! 🚶

Seetrought93 : Shut it, I would tell you to have nightmares, but I suspect you'd love that. Monsters.

WdoBest_84_ : Exactly. That makes it twice. Way to go, champion.

Seetrought93 : Bye.

WdoBest_84_ : 😄

Entry Tuesday

On Monday, I went straight to class and received a message from Liam saying, "So you're finally dating Alina?" and I wonder how things escalated to this point. At the same time, I get a message from Alina saying she told Liam everything, but he misinterpreted it, and now she wants to know if she really needs to correct him. Her message was,

- Are you finally giving a chance to us or not?
- And I replied, "Why not?" with a smiling emoji and there you go.

That's how I found myself in a relationship when the day before I was wondering how to avoid this in the best way at all costs. I told myself that day after, when I could no longer do anything to change the trajectory my life was taking, that this is someone with whom I get along very well and whom I like a lot and care about. So I would do everything to make it work. So that everything goes smoothly, even if it meant going slowly. Without really saying it to her, but she knows me and knows what annoys me, and moreover, she knows I'm a homebody and has never bored me, so there's a good chance I'll manage. That evening, Liam suggested we go celebrate, Liam, Antoine, Alina, Ray, and me. Of course, and we had a little casual game bar since it was the beginning of the week, and that night, Alina and I didn't behave really differently, except for a few kisses here and there; I thought everything was clearly going to go well. My morning fears and worries disappeared. Even though Ray still seemed curious about the situation and thought he'd see how it would evolve, knowing me, and had no comments to make. Typical Ray; I never really know how things work in his head. It seemed to feel completly neutral about the howl thing. The problem is since he knows me the best i would have liked to have a little more of an insiet from him but oh well what can I do about it. He is not someone you can force into doing anything not even talking.

Comment Section

Seetrought93 : That's how my week went.

WdoBest_84_ : I don't understand how you went from "I'm going to tell her no" to "we're a happy couple" in two days.

Seetrought93 : Well, it's simple; I didn't say anything at all, and I'm sure everything will be fine.

WdoBest_84_ : And I think it's all set for me to have a thrilling novel in a few weeks. First date when, again?

Passeureby_102 : 🧍 jerk alert ! 🧍

Seetrought93 : Friday; And who gave yu the right ?

WdoBest_84_ : I can't wait for you to tell me. It's going to be extremely funny.

Seetrought93 : Please, can you support my choices from time to time?

WdoBest_84_ : No, you always make the worst choices. And, to be fair I supported the frist one, the I am not dating her one but you did not follow trought.

Seetrought93 : So pretend.

WdoBest_84_ : Not in the mood; it's much more funny like this.

Seetrought93 : Fine, I give up; I've got no words left.

WdoBest_84_ : I often have that effect on people. But don't fall in love; I'll break your heart.

Seetrought93 : No chances.

WdoBest_84_ : Yeah, that's right; you don't know how to love. But don't worry; with me, it's often supernatural. Or rather worry.

Seetrought93 : Bye.

WdoBest_84_ : Plus, I can't wait to hear all about your date.

Seetrought93 : Yeah, that's right.

WdoBest_84_ : I know you like how direct I am and now you send me less and less comments about it by the way, you're asserting yourself. What great results. I am having thes best impact on you.

Seetrought93 : Hum.

WdoBest_84_ : Bye. Kiss.

The-hot-girt_42 : Again you people talk to much.

Joker-99- : Yes you do !

WdoBest_84_ : If you don't like it kill yourselves.

Passeureby_102 : 🚶 Too much drama here 🚶

Jerom_666_ : And Insane people.

Entry Saturday morning.

So, on Friday, just after it happened. It was the first date, finally the first official one; well, that's what we said. I was a little nervous. I tried to make some effort and everything, but as I'd said, we were still good friends in my mind. The shift was not complete in my head yet. Even if I think on both sides, there were some doubts, no, let's say shyness because it was a different situation you know. It was a nice cinema and dinner date. I just noticed she expected more from me, so I had to be more attentive, more gallant, and say sweet things I guess.

<u>**Comment Section**</u>

WdoBest_84_ : Could you please tell the story properly? You shouldn't have to be told that, right? More details ?

Seetrought93 : I thought you found I gave too many details.

WdoBest_84_ : That doesn't mean you have to stop giving them all together.

Seetrought93 : Whatever.

WdoBest_84_ : So more already.

So here's how it went down exactly. I woke up that morning in quite a good mood, so I suppose I slept well. I yawned, stretched, and took about five minutes to sit up and another ten minutes to completely leave my bed. Then I opened my blinds to make sure I wouldn't go back to bed after having such trouble getting up in the first place.

<u>**Comment Section**</u>

WdoBest_84_ : You think you're incredibly funny, don't you?

Seetrought93 : Well, you wanted details, so I'm going all in; you're going to get all my Friday.

WdoBest_84_ : Shut up and tell me about the date with fewer details. I don't want to know how long the metro ride took you, nor how much people looked at you weirdly or not. Otherwise, I'll track you down and kill you instantly.

Seetrought93 : It's fine. I'll stop teasing you.

WdoBest_84_ : Good.

Seetrought93 : You should see someone for your anger issues.

WdoBest_84_ : Shut up.

Seetrought93 : Okay, okay.

So in the evening, we met in front of the UGC cinema in Bercy to watch a movie she chose, whose title I still can't remember because I fell asleep during it—almost the entire time. It was a horror film, so I couldn't really help but fall asleep when it became a bit too slow with the suspense, the music, and the screams; it's perfect for a nap.

So during the whole walk from the cinema to the restaurant where we were going to eat, she complained about my nap and started to tell me roughly what I missed, but I confess I just pretended to follow because I suppose I saw what I needed to see.

When we arrived, we sat down, ordered cocktails, and appetizers while she continued trying to convince me that the movie was worth it. And that I should maybe try to watch it again.

- What you don't understand is that, actually, it already did its job, making me sleep deeply, lulled by the screams of the actors and even the audience sometimes.
- What a waste, still, you paid a ticket to sleep ?It's not a waste problem. I rarely watch the whole movie when it comes to horror; I only see it entirely if there's really something to think about and torture my mind.
- That was kind of the case. It's a bit complicated to know how it got to that point.
- No, it's basic. Wrong place, wrong time, then sudden madness. No originality; and he's not even really a psychopath; he doesn't have the intelligence or even the stature.
- If you say so.
- Hum, I say so.
- Aside from that, for a first date, you could have faked enjoying the movie.
- That's what I did; I just deeply fell asleep. And enjoyed the nap very much.
- Seriously?
- Well, more seriously, isn't it better for a good relationship that I'm honest?
- Not at the beginning.
- We've known each other for over 8 years; you would know if I were lying.
- We've just started dating; I would notice the effort and be flattered.

Comment Section

WdoBest_84_ : She's right; you should make more of an effort; you wanted to go out with her; you have to put in some work.

Seetrought93 : Stop interrupting me, or I'll stop.

WdoBest_84_ : I'm just using the comment section. You can proceed by ignoring me.

Seetrought93 : Yeah.

WdoBest_84_ : Go on, please.

Seetrought93 : Hum.

So we continued the "argument" I mean fake argument.

- You'd feel flattered if I lied to you. Noted.
- I didn't say it in that way.
- In what way then?
- You know very well what I meant.
- I know ?
- You know what? Forget it; you're annoying me.
- Perfect. So what do you want to eat?
- You're not going to apologize, are you?
- Of course not; I didn't do anything.
- Fine.
- Fine. So what do you want to eat?
- Pizza.
- Yes, which one?
- Hawaiian.
- Bad choice, gross. But it's your choice. I'm going to take a carnivore one, and no exchanges because I don't eat pizza with pineapple.
- No worries.
- Are you going to sulk for long?
- I'm not sulking; I'm just disappointed.
- About what? We agreed that we wouldn't drastically change our behavior.
- Yes, but I thought you would treat me better, my bad for fantasizing about my boyfriend taking more care of me.
- Seriously?
- Yes. I don't feel you engaged already.
- Did you think about if that felt a bit weird for me and if I wanted to take my time to adapt to the change in our relationship?
- Well, I'm in the same situation, and I think I'm managing quite well.
- We are not the same are we are now.
- Okay. We are different, so I'll give you some time to get used to it.
- Thank you.
- But I'm still somewhat annoyed.
- I'm sorry.
- Don't take too long; I think I've already waited too long.
- I'll do my best.
- That's all I ask.

<u>Comment Section</u>

WdoBest_84_ : Not bad; I think you got away with it to easily, but good job.

Seetrought93 : I know, right?

WdoBest_84_ : Don't keep her waiting too long, especially since you didn't get off on the right foot.

Seetrought93 : I care about her; I'll do my best.

WdoBest_84_ : Noted. Good luck. But all that means you're going to become boring.

Seetrought93 : What do you mean?

WdoBest_84_ : People in relationships, especially those who make an effort, are boring.

Passeureby_102 : 🚶 Too much boredome here 🚶

WdoBest_84_ : Oh my god disappear already

WdoBest_84_ : Don't tell me more about dates; I'm already feeling lazy about it, so don't.

Seetrought93 : Okay. I will not tell YOU but I will still write about it if I want to. You just have to skim through it.

WdoBest_84_ : Ugh.

Seetrought93 : 😄

WdoBest_84_ : We'll talk again when you've broken up.

Seetrought93 : Rude.

WdoBest_84_ : And for the arguments in the meantime.

Seetrought93 : You're really annoying;

WdoBest_84_ : I know, and I'm proud of it.

Seetrought93 : Ught.

_ Two weeks later _

Entry Sunday morning.

Her car had finally been freed up, so from then on I started driving sometimes when she was tired. Became more attentive, like writing more often, asking how she was, kissing her, holding her hand, and I had a hard time getting used to it at first, but I eventually managed. For a long time, everything was fine.

Comment Section

WdoBest_84_ : I told you not to bore me with the details of lovers; I want arguments.

Seetrought93 : They suck, and most of the time I come home, not even hearing everything, not even what I respond to.

WdoBest_84_ : What an asshole.

Seetrought93 : I know, but I really can't stand arguments; they bore me easily. I think they put me in a trance" and the version of me that appears well, he is easier for her to deal with because he often agrees with her. Even if later I do whatever I want.

WdoBest_84_ : I see. That's not bad, it's usable material, I think.

With Liam, Antoine, Hannah, André, Alina, and clearly Ray, we decided to take a little vacation in the south of France with the beach and the sun. Everything was organized: the train, the Airbnb, everything. So, we left the friday, right at the start of the holidays to get there. We were all looking forward to relaxing—some more than others, but we won't get into that. The train ride was tiring since everyone was sleeping, so it was clear that tonight we were going for a simple little restaurant and then sleep. And that's what I proposed when we arrived at the apartment.

Okay, but who sleeps where? We only have four rooms and two couples that will definitely want to sleep together. Then I don't know how it's going to work for the other four boys.

- I'll stay with Antoine, and I suppose Ray will be with André.
- That's going to be fun. Said André.
- There are two rooms on the left and two on the right. I suggest that the two couples get laid on their side, and we're calm in ours.
- You're absolutely right; Liam and André and I chose the only room with two beds, which happens to be on the right, sorry.
- No problem.
- Okay, we'll all get changed and meet in the living room to go have dinner?
- Perfect.
- Since there's a shower on each side, it's even more efficient.
- Well, Ryan and I will shower first, is that okay, Alina?
- Yes, yes, it's fine, go ahead; I'm going to take a fake little nap.
- Good idea, me too. *Added Ray yawning*
- You have to keep him from sleeping, he doesn't know what a little nap is; he'll sleep all night, and no one will be able to wake him up.
- I'll handle it Will, *answered André*
- Thanks.

We all went to our rooms to change and freshen up before dinner. And after two hours and thirty minutes, we were sitting at the closest seafood restaurant we could find that still had tables since it was 8:30 PM. I can say that it was long. The fact is that we eventually found a place, and I can say I'm starving.

- I could eat for four people at once; I'm so hungry.
- You impregnate her with triplets, Ryan, good job.
- Shut up, Ray.
- What? I'm just congratulating you.
- Hum.
- So, while we wait for the orders to arrive, I suppose you'll want us to make a little plan for the week, or at least for tomorrow.

- Welcome, the nerdy Antoine.
- Yeah, it's better to wake up when we want, and then we'll see what we feel like doing.
- Well, I wanted to go parasailing, and I was going to suggest that for tomorrow.
- I'm in.
- Me too.
- I don't really want to do that; can't we just go to the beach instead, Will? And let Ray and Antoine figure it out on their own.
- But no, I want to go; it'll be fun. You can just go to the beach; I'll join you later.
- Mmm, whatever you want.
- Okay, household scenes aren't my thing, and the food is here. So, we'll leave tomorrow for tomorrow?
- Okay, Liam. You're jealous because you're all alone, aren't you?
- Speak for yourself, and your little wife was stolen by Alina, and you're upset.
- No, on the contrary, I'm more at peace now that I don't have her constantly in my way.
- I didn't say anything, so I don't know why I'm being attacked.
- I'm sorry, ex-wife.
- Why am I the wife?
- No reason, little brother.
- Damn you.
- Another season of housekeeping. Your polyamorous side is becoming annoying, Will.
- Pffff.
- Anyway, the food is here; we eat, and then we're going to bed.
- Best plan ever, André. Let's do that.

The next morning, when I arrived in the living room, Ray was the only one awake. He was getting ready to go to the pool, which was down in the building we were in. I offered to join him and went to get my stuff in the room to follow him. But when I got there, Alina woke up and stared at me with a questioning look.

- I'm going to the pool with Ray. You can go back to sleep.
- Don't you want to stay and cuddle under the sheets with me?
- No. I'd rather go swimming.
- I see you prefer your husband to your wife. Great.
- Stop, Alina; don't start saying that too; 'she laughed' Come on, I'm going. I'm just going to grab a towel in the bathroom, Okay?

- See you soon.
- See you soon.

As I was about to step out the door, she said to me:

- Don't I get a kiss?
- No. Not until you've brushed your teeth. Sorry.
- Asshole, don't you know about romance?
- No, it doesn't ring a bell. Sorry.

With that, I went out to join Ray. We swam for an hour or two, and then we walked closer to the sea; it was nice, especially to chat a bit.

- So everything is going well with Alina? You generally don't talk about it too much, but I noticed you were anxious about sharing an apartment—or rather a bed—with her for two weeks.
- Yeah, it's a bit new for us. I mean, next-level stuff.
- Hmm. I can understand. And are you ready for that?
- I don't know?
- Are you in love at least?
- Of course, I guess I am; I never really know.
- You are such a waste.
- Come on.
- Fine, but I mean, how is it that you never seem to know when it comes to love, and you just go on hurting people?
- It's not on purpose.
- Yes, but take a break from it, please.
- Why does it seem like you're mad at me particularly about this? It's not like you know better when it comes to love.
- I know more than you, that's for sure.
- Really? I would like to know more about this.
- There's nothing more to tell. Let's go back.
- You're really not going to tell me.
- No.
- Fine, let's go then. But I never knew you had things you never told me. Hmm. Seeing that I looked really hurt, he added: I really can't talk to you about

it right now, but I promise you're the only person I want to tell anyway, so it will come. Soon, I hope.

- So cryptic, okay, I won't ask more questions and will just wait.
- Thank you. Let's go.
- Yes.

So we went back, and on the way we remained silent. When we arrived, it was already 1 PM, and everyone was awake, having breakfast, so we went to join them.

- Good swim session?
- Yeah, we took a little walk too.
- I know we went to look for you, but you weren't there, and on top of that, you had the great idea of leaving your phones here.
- Sorry, Babe. I didn't think of that.
- Clearly.
- Okay, is the drama between Will and his spouses over? Is it possible to eat now in peace?
- Yeah, of course, sorry, Liam; I completely forgot your jealousy issue.
- There's not really anything to be jealous about; sharing is tough. Only Will finds it worthwhile.
- Alina, I said, rolling my eyes. You don't have to be so dramatic; I'm here now, aren't I?
- Yeah, I guess.
- Okay, enough drama. What are we doing today?
- Good question, André; who wants to come chill at the beach with me? First day completely chill and restoring after the suffering that is university.
- Yeah, and that way Ray and I can go parasailing with Antoine. Great idea, babe.
- No, the point isn't to get there and split up; don't you just want to sunbathe on the beach with me?
- Sunbathe? What? I'm already naturally tan.
- He makes a point, but I wouldn't mind sunbathing with you; I even though I don't really need to either. Any chance to do nothing and just watch the sea,
- I'm in.
- Thanks, Hannah. So, Liam, Ryan, André, what do you want to do?
- I'm going to do like Hannah and do nothing today; maybe a little walk on the beach? Chill day.
- I'm going to read a bit on the beach, and we'll see if I'll walk around town a little.

- I'll follow you, André. Maybe I'll meet my summer crush and scope out the best places to go dancing tonight.
- Good idea, Liam, that way you are going to be less annoying. You do need to get laid. After the Tom-Lauren fiasco, you're in one of those moods.
- Thank you very much, Will.
- My pleasure. Besides, you haven't told me exactly what happened, and we'll have to do that.
- Mmm, I don't know if I want to remember, but we'll see later; I need to find something to bite first.

The rest of breakfast was spent deciding at what time everyone would come back to the apartment for dinner together and deciding the end of the evening.

- Consequently, when we got to the beach, the little groups separated according to activities.
- At 6:30 PM sharp, Ray and I were back at the apartment. Antoine had come back earlier, saying, I quote, "I've done enough sports for the day," just after parasailing. What a lazy guy.
- We went inside.
- Cool, there are only Liam and André left; I'll call them to see if they're on their way.
- Okay, I'm going to freshen up. I suppose Alina is in our room.
- Yep.
- I'm going to join her.
- Figured. I turn to Ray, and he looks at me with the same semi-annoyed and lost expression from this morning.
- How's it going, Ray?
- Fine, of course. *And his face becomes normal again.* Nothing at all is going on.

It was the first time I saw him so distracted and distant. I didn't really understand his change in behavior, but I guessed he needed time to talk to me about it. It is a little weird seeing hime like that. I am a little worried.

- Okay. Well, I'm leaving, *I said, showing the way to the room with my thumb.*

Arriving in the room, I see Alina lying on the bed with a book in her hands.

- Hey, I'm back. Did you have a good day?

- Yeah, but not as good as yours, I guess since you just got back. It seems that after living together, you'd have less desire to spend the whole day together, but I guess I was wrong. I'm the only idiot who thinks you would have used the opportunity to spend more time with me. But once again, I was wrong.
- Don't be like this, Alina.
- Like what?
- I didn't notice time passing; we had a great time, and so we came back late.
- It's just the first day; we have two weeks; you absolutely don't need to react like that.
- I suppose and hope so.
- Will kissing you make up for it?
- Not really, but you can always try.
- With pleasure.

I move closer to her and give her a light kiss on the lips.

- So you're not sorry, huh?
- Funny.

She pulls me by the collar of my shirt and kisses me long until we are both out of breath. Then she gives me a mischievous smile and goes back to her book after adding a wink.

- That's more like it.
- Mmm. I'll take a shower.
- Okay, she says without taking her eyes off her book.
- And it's me who doesn't want to spend time with you when you prefer your book.
- You wouldn't dare.
- What, you should suggest following me to the shower not going back to your book.
- We have to go eat with the others in a few minutes.
- In an hour, Liam isn't back yet.
- You don't deserve me to follow you.
- Oh, really? Okay, I'll go by myself then.
- Go ahead.
- Note that I'm pouting.
- Kid.

I enter the shower, pretending to pout, but a few minutes later, she joins me, and I feel like everything is forgiven. I feel it very well, if you know what I mean.When we get out of the shower and our room, Liam has finally come back, and everyone seems ready to go eat. Most importantly, he brought a plan for the evening. We were to join some new friends he made at a dancing bar. Which we did. When we arrived around 11 PM, there weren't many people yet, and his friends were already there; they seemed to be about the same age as us. We went over to them, and he introduced us.

- So here's Brian and Sam, who I met this morning and who are also on vacation here. And, Brian, Sam, here are my friends, Antoine, Will, Ray, Alina, Hannah,
- André, and Ryan. Sam actually studies at our unie. Great coincidence right ?
- Nice to meet you, we all said with smiles.

After the introductions, we all sat down and went around the table to see what everyone was doing and our ages, the basic info, and I confirm they are in the same age group as us; I feel like we're going to spend a lot of time together during the next few weeks. As the evening went on, I felt a closeness between Ray and Brian that only intensified over the time we spent with them during the holidays.By the end of the week, I think I did most of the activities, if not all, that could be considered exciting, and I did so mostly with Antoine and Ray. Sometimes Alina, if she caught up with our schedule and or didn't feel lazy. Also, we often met Brian at those activities; that was quite nice at first, and I noticed Ray seemed less "dark" like when we arrived, which I liked a lot. However, Alina didn't really like that I was having a lot of fun without her and insisted that we spend more time just the two of us. And we were still in one of those stupid arguments about romance or more precisely, a lack of romance on my part:

- Are you listening to me?
- Yeah, but I find that you're repeating yourself, and I'm worried about you.
- Do you think this is the time to make a joke?
- I'm serious; I'm really worried.
- William.
- Full name, huh.
- Are you going to take this conversation seriously in the end? I'm not joking, seriously.
- I know, but we've already had it, and we spent almost the whole day together the day before yesterday.
- Maybe, but not alone, and you were completely into your stupid contest with Ray; you barely gave me the time of the day, and you call that spending time together,

and you spent almost the whole day today outside; I'd like us to spend time just the two of us; is that possible for you? Or do you think I am asking too much of you.
- No.
- Thank you.
- You want to have dinner just the two of us tonight and then walk on the beach? Romantic enough for you? *I said, moving closer to her since she was sitting on the bed and I was standing in front of her. Then, I sat next to her and grabbed her hand.* Hey, I'm sorry; I didn't understand exactly what you were saying last time. I'll really make more of an effort, I promise.
- Okay for tonight, are you going to tell them?
- Yes, I'm going. *I give her a light kiss on the lips and leave the room.*

The second week is somewhat going better, but from time to time, it seems that I'm not doing enough, and it's already the last day, and we're going to spend it all at the beach doing everything and nothing at the same time, and it's simple and great; in the evening we planned to stroll through the little ephemeral market that opened the day before. In short, a good ending for the first part of the vacation. And despite the little arguments, it was a good evening, and we returned to Paris completely rested and ready to continue the vacation, each on our side. Liam, Antoine, Ray, and I are returning to Bordeaux three days after coming back to Paris.

The three days in Paris passed with Alina constantly harassing me to stay with her in our apartment or hers for the rest of the vacation instead of going back:

- I'm leaving tonight at 5 PM; do you still think I'm going to change my mind? At this point, even you should know that it's dead.
- Really, you want us to be appart for three weeks? *she said, pouting and following me everywhere while I finished packing my suitcase.*
- Yep.
- Are you not going to miss me, even just a little?
- No, not at all.
- Hmm. So you really don't want to spend time with me. It's becoming clearer over time.
- Alina !
- What? Even when we're together, you prefer something else, so I'm sure now that being alone with me is going to bore you to death.
- Are you done? Because I'd like to grab something to eat and take a nap before catching the train since I don't really sleep well on public transport. *I give her a*

light kiss on the lips and start changing my t-shirt to go out; she stands in front of me and gives me a look, like to say, you asshole, I want to kill you.
- Is that your answer to what I said?
- Yes. I'm hungry; are you coming to eat with me?
- No. I'd prefer to go home.
- Okay.
- What, are you serious? You can't wait to be away from me, can you?
- Alina, please. I just want to eat, rest, and leave peacefully without all this. *I said, walking past her to head to the front door.*
- Are you leaving?
- Yeah, I'm going to get something to eat.

At that moment, the front door opens, and it's Ray who comes in after doing his last-minute shopping.

- Oh, you're back?
- Yep, I'm going to finish my suitcase. I brought food; I'm sure you're starving.
- Sure, you're the best; I can always count on you.
- Of course, little brother.
- Hmm. I am not saying anything this time because you brought food.
- You're really not saying anything ?
- No, I'm way too hungry.
- Cool, I prefer that. *I stick my tongue out at him and call him an asshole, but he keeps laughing, that jerk.*
- Mmm, all of this is my belly's fault; otherwise, I would have killed you.
- Mmm. *I stick my tongue out at him again.*

At that moment, he notices Alina behind me, so he turns to her and says:

- Do you want to eat with us? I'm sure Will doesn't want to share this gluttony, but who cares, right?
- No, I am leaving.
- Really, you don't want to eat?
- No. I'm going to go since he clearly doesn't want me here.
- Alina, I didn't say that.
- No, but you thought it so hard that it's like you were saying it.
- I'm sorry.

- You're not denying it; that's already good. I'm going to go home and rest. We'll see each other when you return; I'm tired, anyway, and that's what you want right ?
- It's for the best. *I move closer to her, but when I try to touch her, she dodges and heads for the door quickly. She opens it, steps out, and closes it behind her without looking back.*

I know this time I really hurted her, and I have serious apologies to give, but I felt relieved she was gone, and I didn't want to argue anything at all now. I was fed up with arguments. I hate arguments.

- What was that about?

I turn to Ray, who is looking at me attentively.

- Care to explain?
- No.
- Let's eat then.
- Okay. And thank you for not asking.
- Always, little brother.
- Dick.
- Hmm. You love me.
- I do not.
- Hmm.

The rest of the day goes well, and when we arrived in Bordeaux, I go straight to bed. Tomorrow is another day, as they say.

<u>**Comment Section**</u>

WdoBest_84_ : I just read what you wrote during your two weeks of vacation. They weren't very restful, tell me.

Seetrought93 : No, not at all.

WdoBest_84_ : But I also think you prefer to spend time with others, especially Ray, rather than your girlfriend.

Seetrought93 : But it's just that with her I feel squeezed and obliged to make too much effort. It's annoying and not relaxing at all.

WdoBest_84_ : That's a relationship that will lead to marriage.

Seetrought93 : Fuck you.

WdoBest_84_ : I love you too.

WdoBest_84_ : It'll be fine, don't worry.

Seetrought93 : You think?

WdoBest_84_ : Yeah, you're going to break up soon; I'm sure of it.

Seetrought93 : You know what? I'm really going to go to bed.

WdoBest_84_ : Good night, sweetheart.

Seetrought93 : Yeah, right.

WdoBest_84_ : Wait it was the first time you were going away with a girlfriend right ?

Passeureby_102 : 🚶 Big Fat jerk alert ! 🚶

Seetrought93 : Yeah. And you, please dont come here again.

WdoBest_84_ : Showed.

The-hot-girl_42 : Yeah you should stay single indefinitely.

_ Five days later _

Entry Friday night.

I haven't heard from Alina even the next day or in the three or four days that followed. I stayed at home and spent the beginning of the holidays mainly lounging around my parent's house, chatting about everything and anything, or just annoying her.

Ray had dinner at home almost every day, and my mom couldn't be happier. In short, the routine was fine until this Thursday evening when I found myself on the phone with a very angry Alina, and the worst part is that I don't quite understand why because I'm sure I haven't done anything in the last four days to make her angry, and that's exactly what I tell her.

- I haven't done anything, so why are you calling me so on edge?
- Exactly, you've done absolutely nothing. Nothing at all, nada.
- I'm not sure I understand.
- I don't write to you or call you for a few days, and you don't even seek to know if I'm doing well.
- Well, I thought you were busy, and if you needed something, you would write to me.
- That's exactly the problem. You never seek me out; I am never on your mind.I'm always the one who wants to talk to you first or spend time together. When I don't, we don't talk. How does that happen?
- Well, I don't know; it's always been like this, and you didn't seem to have a problem with it before.
- Yes, because I thought you'd improve, that you'd be more interested with time, with the feelings that would stard bulding up, but it seems there are no feelings to establish. I don't know what to do, and with what you told me last time, I feel like I'm starting to bore you, and you won't wait long to throw me away. Am I wrong?
- Alina.
- Am I wrong?
- Yes, obviously. *I hear a sigh of relief escape her at the other end of the line.*

I'm sitting in my room, on my bed, and I'm looking closely at her words, and I don't know why I feel my heart tighten. It's exactly because I thought something like this would happen, and that's why I didn't want to date a friend I cared about. I don't really know what I should do and what I feel. I just know I don't want to hurt her and that I care far too much for her. I really don't want to lose her. I sigh in turn, get up, and go to the window to breathe in some outside air.

- Alina, are you still there? *I said, noticing she hasn't said anything for a while now.*
- Yes. I don't really know what to say.
- You don't have to say anything. I'm going to make this work; I'll improve, I promise. I'll take the time I'm going to spend here to think and find a solution; I promise you.
- No, we should do it together.

- It's coming from me, so I'll handle it. *I sigh again and add:* I'm going to have to let you go; Ray's parents came back from vacation yesterday, so I'm going over there for dinner, and it wouldn't be polite to be late.
- Yes, of course you have something with Ray.
- What does that mean?
- Nothing, have a good evening, Will; I have better things to do too.
- Alina, it's not... *Before I could finish my sentence, she had already hung up.*

The rest of the evening was uneventful, but the next day my mom called me to the living room after dinner with a slightly more serious look than usual.

- Come sit near me, *she said, smiling and patting the place on the couch right beside her.*
- Okay? *I said, sitting in the said spot.* So what's going on, mom?
- Nothing, I just want to ask how your life and studies are going. In short, how are you?
- We talked about it when I arrived; everything is fine. *I scratch my head and look at her, tilting my head sideways and raising an eyebrow.* What do you think I should add, be clearer.
- Very well. What's going on with your girlfriend, Alina?
- Oh, that.
- Yes.
- How can you know things aren't going well?
- Because I have you in my business every day, and I haven't seen you smile while texting someone or spending hours on the phone, so I find that you really don't have the behavior of someone who has a girlfriend or at least one that he gets along with.
- You have an eye.
- You're my baby; obviously. And besides, yesterday when you got her call, you didn't really seem to jump for joy.
- Mhm. *That was all I could come up with as a response. I didn't really know what to say; I was still lost myself.*
- So tell me what's going on?
- I don't know where to start.
- I'm tempted to say you should start at the beginning, but I know you too well, and you're likely to tell me all the days of your relationship in detail, and I'll end up confused, *she said, laughing slightly, which made me smile too.*

- A little harsh, mom.
- But true. Well, I want a simple little summary sentence.
- I find that she is too present in my life, and she thinks I'm not present enough in hers. Not involved enough in the relationship. But I'm doing my best.
- I said one sentence.
- Fine. Just take the first.
- What was it again?
- Mom.
- I'm just joking to get you to relax a bit.
- It works like always.
- I know.
- So what do you think?
- I think you're probably wrong in this story. I'm sure of it, actually.
- Mom. *I said, putting some space between us by sliding a little to the right.* You should be on my side.
- Not really. But seriously, if you look at things from a cold and outside perspective, do you think you spend a lot of time with her, especially on your own initiative?
- Honestly, no.
- Why?
- Because I don't necessarily feel like it.
- And do you think that's normal?
- Not really.
- And what do you conclude from that?
- I'm not sure, mom.
- I'm sure you know, even if you may not be ready to accept it yet.
- I really don't know.
- Just think about it, sweetheart.
- Okay.
- Well, do you want to watch a movie with me?
- What a swift change of subject *I said, scooting closer to her again to rest my head on her shoulder. She smiles tenderly at me and turns to the TV.*
- So, what do you want to watch?
- Where's dad?
- He's in our bedroom; I think he's reading.
- Okay.

- So?
- I'll let you choose.
- A detective movie, then.
- I expected nothing less from you.
- I know I'm the best.

She chooses a detective movie, and we watch it together, laughing and trying to investigate on our side. I smile the whole time, but what she told me lingers in my head. I know the answer deep down inside.

The rest of my vacation at home goes well, even if I have the same problem in the back of my head. Mostly, since I'm such an adult, I ignore all Alina's calls. I'm very mature. I'm proud of myself too.

_ A few days later _

Entry Sunday morning.

I'm quietly sitting in my room brooding and blaming myself. Clearly the daily routine of Will. I hear the door to my room open, but I don't move; I stay lying on my bed and stare at the ceiling with great interest. Ray comes to lie down next to me and doesn't say anything for a while, then he throws me a :

- That bad, hun?
- Yep.
- How are you managing?
- I don't know. I'm both relieved and sad.
- So you made the right choice.
- I know.
- Time will probably improve the rest.
- I hope so.

He doesn't respond and we remain silent for the rest of the evening. Then he orders us some kebabs through deliveroo, and we have dinner in the living room, still without talking. He suggests watching a horror movie; I agree, and we spend the rest of the evening in front of the TV. It was exactly what I needed—no talking and just spending a quiet evening. I didn't need to tell him anything. He already knows the essentials, and he doesn't really need to know the rest.

- I gather up my courage and finally call Alina.
- Hello, how are you?
- Seriously, you've been ignoring me for over two weeks, and you come out with a hello how are you?
- I'm sorry.
- I hope you are, but I'm not sure that's enough.
- I know. I talked a lot about it with my mom and...
- You did what? I'm glad to see you're discussing it, but I would have liked you to do it with me.
- I know, but I needed a break to catch my breath.
- So we were on a break. I just didn't get the memo.
- You know what I mean by that.
- No, exactly, I don't know. I don't even remember why we're arguing. And besides, what's the conclusion of your break? Did you feel better during your break, and do you not want to get out anymore?
- Alina.
- Did you miss me, even just a little?
- Of course, I did.
- Glad to hear. Otherwise, why are we arguing exactly? Am I asking too much of you, or have you grown tired of me?
- I'm tired of arguing.
- You took a break for two weeks, though. Wasn't that enough?
- Clearly not.
- I'm still too clingy, then. I didn't call you when I saw you weren't responding to my calls.
- Alina.
- What?
- I'm fed up, and so are you.
- Don't decide what I feel.
- Aren't you tired?
- Yes, but not of you; more of the fact that you don't really want to move in the same direction as me. What do I need to do for you to show me interest?
- Nothing.
- What does that mean?
- That there's nothing to do.
- But still.

- Let's stop here, Alina.
- What?
- You understood me well. We're hurting each other, and that's not what I want.
- And what I want counts?
- Yes, of course.
- Then I don't want to stop anything at all at the risk of being clingy again.
- Alina !
- Stop using my name as a weapon. If you want to break up with me, be clear; don't make me do all the work just to give you an excuse or reason.
- I want to break up.
- I didn't expect you to be so blunt.
- Alina!
- I said to stop with my name. *Her voice had risen, and she was now yelling through the phone.*
- I'm sorry.
- Yeah, you are, aren't you?
- I'm going to hang up; I think that's best.

She didn't respond, but I heard sobs instead. This made me stay connected, unsure of how to respond. Eventually, she hung up after a little while. I have never felt so bad about a break up before. What I just did was selfish but I also felt relieved and bad for being so.

I lay down on my bed, eyes fixed on the ceiling, not knowing what else to say.

Liam helped me a lot to send my feelings and my emotions to Alina without talking to her directly because I had asked him to, and it helped to know that she could complain about me to him after having hurt her so much.

_ Three weeks after the return _

Entry Thursday.

That week I was really bored; I needed to entertain myself; I spent my time feeling guilty about what happened with Alina; then I had my finals, so I wanted to have fun. And, apart from my friends at university, I hadn't seen my other friends like Liam or Antoine for a while, even though we had the best evenings together, so I thought I would call him to go out on Friday night, and maybe even stay at his place afterward since Ray had gone back to his uncle's and I was too lazy to be in an empty apartment.So I call him:

- Hey Liam, it's been a while; how's it going?
- I'm fine; I just finished my finals, and I want to die, but it's not that big of a deal.
- Oh, you just finished too?
- You know we're all at university and that it's always the same periods, don't you?
- No, but generally, you finish before I do.
- Yeah, that's true; I didn't choose a job as complicated as yours to create things.
- Shut up.
- Fine.
- So do you want to celebrate the end of the mental torture this Friday night? I'm sure you're not too tired for one of our legendary nights.
- Hahaha, you mean a break? We haven't finished our studies yet.
- You get what I mean, don't you?
- Yes, yes.
- So?
- I can't this Friday; I have something during the entire weekend.
- Damn it.
- Next week, rain check?
- Why not. Let's keep in touch.
- Cool.

I admit I was a bit disappointed, but I thought I'd ask Antoine to come with me or go out with my university friends that night since they had proposed it earlier. Antoine was also very busy, so I ended up calling Marc, who was my partner in most of the group projects at university, to tell him that I would join them at the new bar they wanted to try that day.

<u>**Comment section :**</u>

WdoBest_84_ : You haven't written much lately.

Seetrought93 : Yeah, the beginning of classes and my internship are killing me. I'm buried under work right now.

WdoBest_84_ : Sorry to hear that

Entry from the following Saturday evening

As Friday night arrived, I got ready wearing a simple assemble "jeans and a t-shirt" and joined Marc and the others in front of a dance bar called Kaos. From the outside, you could get a sense of the atmosphere, and it was at its peak. I waved to Marc, and we all went inside together. It was dark, but full of colorful neon lights everywhere, like any respectable dance bar. The bar was all the way to the left, stretching along the wall, and there were four bartenders behind, all very busy given the influx of orders. The place was packed.

The restrooms and coat check were located upstairs, and just to the right of the bar, there was another room for dancing and another bar at the far end with two equally busy bartenders this time.

Along the walls in both the first and second rooms, there were couches to sit on and small low tables in front.

We settled around one of those tables, and I suggested getting the first round—shots rhum flavored, of course—two per person, which made twelve since there were six of us.

We were in the second room, but I headed to the bar in the first room, thinking I might get served faster. When I arrived there, I did my best to catch the attention of one of the bartenders; it was a blonde with very nice hair, wearing jeans and a blue t-shirt.

She smiled at me and asked what I wanted.

- You don't really look like a bartender.
- I hear that often, as if not having piercings or tattoos is a crime. But if you want to know everything, I have a butterfly tattooed above my butt and a piercing in my belly button.
- I feel reassured; tonight's cocktails wouldn't be bad. *I said faking a sight of relief.*
- So if I understand correctly, a bartender's skills lie in their style?
- Clearly.
- I see. Otherwise, another way to check if I'm skilled enough for my job would be to examine my entire body. I also hear that good bartenders are good in bed.
- I think that's something I'm willing to verify.
- So what can I get you? *she said with a smile.*

- Twelve shots of rum.
- Right away.

While she was serving me, I turned to the dance floor to watch people dance. And to my surprise, I saw Alina, Antoine, and Liam laughing and dancing right in front of me. A wave of fury and a feeling of betrayal and sadness washed over me, and to block it, I took six of the twelve shots that had just been served. This helped me contain my rage.

- Six more shots, please.
- Okay.
- I'll pay by credit card.

After paying, I returned to my table; we toasted and I acted as if nothing had happened.But the evening wasn't great, and I ended up going home with the pretty bartender without any desire to do so.

Needless to say, the next day when Ray saw her coming out of the guest room as we got home, it was weird. I did my best to get her out as quickly and gently as possible, promising to call her, which I had no intention of doing.

I had a hangover, and I can't say I was really thinking clearly. The mess of my life. Ray was talking behind me and saying things. But I can't tell you now what he said to me because that day, I was completely lost, and I didn't get nearly enough sleep that night for obvious reasons, and I had drank a lot too.

PART 2

Three Months Later

Entry Wednesday

I opened the door, and the first thing that caught my eye was the large red couch in the middle of the room. It was big, imposing, and took up most of the space in the room. The rest of the room was decorated quite simply. There were long beige curtains drawn in front of the three windows behind the couch, a beautiful simple wood desk made of mahogany, and it had an armchair. It was a rocking chair, both black, on either side of the couch. I entered and closed the door behind me, and that was when I noticed for the first time, being so occupied in detailing the room, Dr. Parker, who was sitting behind her desk, observing me intently.

- Hello, Mr. Blanchard.
- Um, *I cleared my throat and timidly replied:* Uh, just call me William.
- Certainly. So, William, what do you think of my couch? I noticed it has captured your attention.
- Indeed, quite a bold choice for a psychiatrist's office, I think, Dr. Parker.
- I know, it doesn't really create a neutral environment, but I've always thought that blood red is a magnificent color, and it is, after all, my favorite color, especially since it is my office where I spend most of my time. I should have something I like right ? Also it is a great discussion opener! You just experienced it first hand.
- Indeed, and I agree with you, it is a beautiful color.
- Thank you. Do you want to try it out? It's as comfortable as it looks.
- Thank you, Dr. Parker.
- My pleasure.

As I hesitantly walked toward the couch, she got up and walked lightly and steadily toward the couch. Once we were both settled, she grabbed the pen that was clipped to the pocket of her open shirt on the upper left and took a small notebook to jot down notes. Then she turned her gaze toward me and smiled.

–   So, what brings you here today, William?

–   Where should I start?

–   The beginning, as is customary.

–   Of course.

–   But first, introduce yourself and then tell me exactly what the problem is that has brought you to me.

–   Well, my name is William Smith, I'm 22 years old, I'm an architecture student, and I am addicted to being seen during sex.

–   Alright. Now, before going further, what is your family situation?

–   I am the eldest son in a family of three children. I have a sister and a brother who are 18 years old, and they are twins. My father is a real estate agent and has his own firm in the south of France in Bordeaux, and my mother is a housewife.

–   What makes a young man from a family that seems so balanced think he is a sex addict and feel the need to talk about it?

–   I am bisexual.

–   But still?

–   My mother is a devout Christian, which, unfortunately, makes her homophobic.

–   I see, and you struggle to accept your sexuality because you feel you are disappointing her?

–   *I lowered my head and said in a small voice,* I am already disappointing her.

–   Do you put a lot of pressure on yourself?

–   To be completely honest... Yes. Well, I'm not sure if it's really bad pressure. It's just that the way I was raised *I said, breathing erratically.* There was an unspoken rule, or rather something specific that was just not openly said, that the eldest had to take care of... well, that he had to take care of his siblings, had to succeed, had to accomplish things and everything... And even though my parents were very loving, very protective, and always told me to do whatever I liked, whatever interested me, I always thought it was my duty to succeed and go far, to help my parents to the best of my ability, and to always be an example. So, yes, in every way, I put pressure on myself, but it's a good pressure. It is just that I am so proud and happy to have my family that I always want to do my best for them. Nothing too... I mean, nothing very traumatic or... *I said, laughing nervously,* I mean, hum There you go. I already started rambling great.

–   So why do you think you are addicted to being seen while having sex? What could make such a charming young man like you, without any major family problems, lose himself in this way? I'm sure that if you talked to your mother, you could confess your bisexuality to her one day and she would... well, she wouldn't have a problem with it at all.

- I completely understand your point of view, Doctor, but it's just that I know my mother. She is actually the person I am closest to since she was a stay-at-home mom; she was always there, took us to school, picked us up, and really took care of us with a lot of love and a lot of patience. And since she is from Africa and was really very religious, she has always wanted to instill the word of God in us. Even if I can't say that I am as pious as she is, I do believe in God... Well, I am not a practicing Christian like she is. I know that her faith has always been so important to her that I have always wanted to do my best to follow it. But I believe I have always had a certain jealousy of God because it has always been this faith that distanced her from me, and I couldn't confide in her; I couldn't tell her who I was completely. Can you imagine seeing someone who means so much to you, who is so close to you, who knows all your sides but to whom you can't tell an important part of you out of fear of losing them? Forever? I believe that's it; that fear of losing her made me lead my life in that way. That I always separated that part of myself. I behaved... I always behaved as if I were someone who is heterosexual, someone who is only interested in girls. I introduced her to several of my girlfriends, girls I was close to, I told her how I felt when I met them, when I saw them, what they made me feel. But each time, I realized that my eyes were fixed on a... *I said, exhaling* My eyes were on a man. *At that moment, I was breathing heavily; I had difficulty breathing so I fell silent for a moment.* At that moment *I said, sighing, I breathed deeply.* Every time I met a guy I liked, who interested me, for whom I had a crush, I forced myself to be silent; I blocked myself, I locked myself... I closed my heart, I blocked it, I forbade myself to dare to feel something that could... *I started to cry,* hurt her. And because I didn't want to hurt her, I never wanted to be the person who could break her heart, who could make her feel any pain whatsoever because she sacrificed so much for me, because she did so much for me, *I continued to cry.* Because she has always been there for me, she has always been my best friend for my whole life. I always... I always held back. Maybe I met... well, when I finally started living in Paris, I could meet guys, be interested in them, flirt a little, but I never went very far; I never allowed myself to let go of that side of myself. Until that fateful day. *I was having trouble breathing.*

- Take your time; you can breathe, calm down, focus on that moment and tell me what happened, taking your time. By telling me exactly what happened.

—   Do you know, to ensure I never stray from my that path a chose for myself I decided no one not even my friends would know about my sexuality. I tought burying it would make it disappear for good.

I inhale So I... I... It was one evening. I remember very well, a Friday night. My friends called me in the afternoon, and they told me they wanted to go to a nightclub to dance, drink, well, in a nusthell, hang out and have some fun, you know, what young people do at our age. So, I accepted. I came back from the office where I was doing my internship, I went home, took a little nap until 10 PM, then I woke up, had a quick little dinner, a sandwich on the go, got dressed, went out, and met up with my friends... I found my friends at one of their places. I forgot to mention that I live with my best friend, so he and I went to a small party at my friend's house, whose name is Adrien, and then we simply took the subway and went straight to a dance bar. Everything was fine; we danced, we drank, a normal evening. Then this young man approached me. He was brown-haired, with hazel eyes, a charming smile. He was wearing a simple red t-shirt with white shorts and simple sandals on his feet. He smiled at me intensely, and I returned his smile. Then he got closer to me and started dancing, rubbing against me. We both found it normal that he was flirting with me, and I flirted back without any problem. As usual. Then at some point, I felt that I needed to go to the restroom, so I pushed him away and headed directly toward the toilets. I didn't see that he was following me until... when I reached the entrance, he turned me around and pushed me against the door. I didn't realize... I didn't realise what was happening until his lips suddenly crashed against mine. He kissed me first softly, then more and more quickly and more and more forcefully as if he had been waiting to do it for a while, might have been the truth. He continued rubbing himself on me and forced my mouth open for him so he could introduce his tongue and mine to kiss me deeply... I remember that at that moment I felt invaded by a strange feeling of... I felt like I was doing something bad, something dirty, that I wasn't allowed to do what I had promised myself never to do for my mother, so I pushed him away violently and tried to get into the restroom. When I entered, there were several doors; I went into one of the stalls to do my usual business. But I didn't notice that he had followed me, but he did, and he pushed me roughly behind the door, and he didn't completely close it behind him. He looked at me and said, Why are you acting shy now when you've been teasing me all evening? Maybe it's time to take responsibility for your actions. You've teased me; you have to take care of it.

I replied: At what point did we sign a contract? He smiled, got closer, put his hands on either side of my head, on my cheeks, and kissed me again. At that moment, I... I widened my eyes when his lips landed on mine, and I noticed that someone had just entered the restroom and noticing us came closer and then had their eyes fixed on us. So I... at first, I was horrified to see that someone saw me doing something I had sworn never to do, but afterward, I *taking a short breath* felt something I had never felt before. The fact of noticing that there was someone in the room next door who saw me kiss another guy while it was something I had forbidden myself to do, that I had forbidden myself to be, even if that was part of me. At that moment, I felt overwhelmed by a feeling that was unknown to me, a kind of unhealthy joy that I couldn't understand at that point. I still don't understand. That look aimed at me, seeing me do something I had hidden my whole life, that gaze of a stranger who met me, who was the first person who knew me completely. I would carry that look with me my whole life because it was that look that pushed me to continue and let go as if it was that look that touched me and not the person in front of me. So, I let myself lean against the wall behind me, let myself be kissed on the neck, on the Adam's apple. He took off my t-shirt and began kissing my chest, and my nipples were hardening at a glance without my gaze ever leaving the green-gray eyes that were behind the door. He started stroking my chest slowly, then reached my zipper and unbuttoned my pants and undid the zip. And, without letting me prepare myself, he seized me in his hand without taking off my boxers at first, but then he plunged his hand in and initially grabbed it with a powerful grip before starting to stroke me more gently, which made me grunt softly. I felt he was satisfied with his effect, but my gaze hadn't changed direction, and even though I felt myself blushing with embarrassment, I continued to look him straight in the eyes and appreciate the effect we had on each other. He completely lowered my pants and boxers and tried to turn me against the wall, but I resisted. He looked at me questioningly. But without a word, I placed myself against the wall on my left side in such a way as to always keep my gaze fixed on the outside toward our onlooker . He saw no downside, took a condom from his pocket behind him, and barely had he lowered his zipper when he took my hand and placed it on his asking me to masturbate him, which I did while always looking toward the door toward the unknown person who was watching us and who didn't seem to be blinking or did we blink at the same time? I had absolutely no idea... Meanwhile, he stroked my entrance sensually, groaning louder and louder. Although I heard my companion's groans of pleasure, I could see the lust and the pleasure gradually rise in the gaze fixed on me, which made me even happier and more excited than the movements of my partner behind me. This made my gaze completely lose itself in his, and so without warning or that I wasn't prepared for, the young man behind me entered me without ceremony, which made me let out a small cry of pain mixed with excitement, and it was the first time I closed my eyes to try to regain my composure before reopening them and noticing that the observer had left, but I didn't know where. I was slightly saddened by that. My partner began to thrust, and when we were finished, I got dressed after cleaning myself up, and I came out to join my friends and tell them I was going home. After that episode, I just returned in automatic mode home because I didn't recognize my own actions, and I felt lost and ashamed among them. At home, I took a hot shower and went to my bed and cried from shame all night long, thinking about the shame and disgust my actions would have inspired in my family if they had gotten wind of it.I stayed in my bed staring at the ceiling without having any idea of what had come over me. I looked at the ceiling, but instead of the beige paint I saw the green-gray eyes that were fixed on me, and when I closed my eyes, I saw them more clearly. I don't know how long I stayed staring at the ceiling because closing my eyes was worse, but the fact is that all that time I felt full of shame and disgust. I must have fallen asleep surely still with that feeling. I didn't allow myself to think or analyze my actions from that evening later because I promised myself to erase them and not think about them as if they were the fruit of one of my darkest nightmares.

After relaying this episode, I opened my eyes because I had to close them to concentrate on my feelings and emotions of that day in order to recount them as clearly as possible and above all to recount them entirely without feeling embarrassed at Dr. Parker's gaze, which was still fixed on me. So, when I opened my eyes, Dr. Parker had put her notebook down on the table beside her, had moved closer by sitting on the edge of her black armchair, and was looking at me with a soft, calm gaze that reassured me immediately. I was certain now that she wouldn't judge me for my dirty actions. Although thinking back, that is an integral part of her job not to show her opinions. She spoke and said to me:

- I'm glad you took the initiative to tell me what you have identified as the beginning of your discomfort. Now I want you to take a notebook or journal and write down without omitting any details what happened next and what brought you to come and talk to me today.

- Very well.
- But before wrapping up the session, you told me what you remembered feeling that day and how you didn't want that to happen again. But if you had to tell me how you really feel now about that day, what would it be?
- Well, as you said, it was my trigger, but above all, I don't see that day as shameful anymore, but rather as the day I realized that by lying to myself and to my parents, I had merely postponed an inevitable deadline when I was going to explode because it would have been impossible for me to keep a false identity my entire life. That day, I realized that by hiding a part of my personality every time to protect myself, in fact, instead of really protecting my parents, I had made my life a big lie while I always said I hated lying. Because while that was happening, I didn't immediately feel shame—no, I felt instead a happiness, or rather a huge joy because for once, I felt seen completely for who I really was. I was kind of, being myself I don't know if it make sense. And I think that's what exacerbated the feeling of shame that followed.
- Well, I am satisfied with this session; I am impressed by the progress made, and even though you are ashamed, you haven't hidden anything from me, and I am delighted. That will help us in the long run. It means you are really here to move forward and heal. Also that you thrust me.
- Thank you, Doctor.
- Writing will allow you to no longer have to reorganize your feelings as you have just done or to embellish them by taking one side rather than the other. But it will allow you to say directly what comes immediately to mind to have a more accurate idea of your emotions and actions. Write everything, every little detail. Is that good for you?
- Yes !
- And, do not worry I am not reading anything you don't want me to.
- Ok.
- Also just to clarify I think One session once a week on wednesdays of 45 minutes could be a good start. What do you think ?
- It is fine.
- Perfect !
- Yes, thank you.
- Have a nice day!
- And you too.

The session had drained me, and all I wanted to do was put that episode aside and refocus on myself and rest. I didn't want to think about all the traumatism still felt due to that episode. I just wanted to go home and get in bed without showering because I was feeling lazy. And I pushed my memories aside. Then I thought that if Ray had been there, he would have asked me how it went, and I would have smiled and said everything was fine while hiding my true emotions as usual, something I need to work on, and I would have told him about the journal I had to write, and he would have asked me if I wanted to go out to get one with him and take the opportunity to fill the fridge; and I would have accepted even if I was lazy, and we would have eaten, and I would have already felt better because I wouldn't have had to think about the state of my life at that moment. But he wasn't there because we had violently argued a week earlier, and he had gone to stay at his uncle's.

So, I just slept for the rest of the day and got up the next day even more tired, but I forced myself to get out of bed, take a shower, and brush my teeth before sitting back on my bed and noticing my laptop that I had left opened after using it that laid on all my stuff and sheets of drawings. I got up to make a small fruit salad, then I returned to my desk with the laptop in front of me, the salad on my left, and thus began

I realized just now that I never told what really happened that made me want to write here. It is so simple and stupide but still too hard on me.

It was a tuesday, I was coming home with some groceries because I had a specific craving and when I entered the house Ray was on the phone.

I put the groceries down to go to my room and change before cooking. When, I tried to get in my room he stopped me and put the phone on speaker.

- Mum Will just got back home, you were asking about him.
- Oh yeah William dear how have you been doing? and your studies?
- Everything is alright although I feel a little swamped.
- I get that but push through it. You are almost done. Both of you.
- Don't bother worrying about Ray, he is never bothered, himself. It feels like everything is too easy for him.
- It kind of is.
- That's my little genius. Oh and I almost forgot, how about the dating side. William, a serious girlfriend ? And Ray my baby, à girlfriend, à boyfriend, both ?
- No such thing for either of us mum.

- Oh come on make a little effort to meet someone Ray. I want to see what your taste is like. You never brought anyone serious home, come on.
- I will try harder, mum. We have to go, it is time to cook, talk to you later.
- Ok baby ! Good night boys.
- Good night we said together before he hung up.
- What are we cooking ?
- I don't know as you wish I don't have any idea.
- What about the groceries you brought ? I thought you had a craving.
- Oh yeah pasta and bolognese.
- Oh ok I will start on it you can go change. Are you okay you seem out of it out of a sudden.
- Oh no no I was remembering something from class today that I wanted to read again. I am going to change and come back.
- Ok !

I really was not ok. Just that little distinction his mom made, and my mood dropped completely. I wasn't even hungry anymore. When I closed the door behind me tears started falling down on my cheeks.

I am sure you don't get what I am talking about. It was that simple sentence. " William, a serious girlfriend ? And Ray, a girlfriend, a boyfriend, both ? " I felt like I was less in that moment, less than myself. I wanted so bad to be acknowledged at that moment, the whole me. Realizing that I will never get to be asked that precise question, ever, because of my own choices well it was hard to accept.

Also by my own doing I had no one to confide in and it sucked even more. It was such a simple sentence, a simple and innocent question brought me my knees and there was nothing I could do because it was my own choice.

It took me a while to get hold of myself, change, and leave the room. By the time I was out, Ray was pretty much done.

- I am sorry it took so much time
- No worries. Are you sure everything is alright ?
- Hum !
- You look a little sad. Sure you don't want to talk about it ?
- No it is okay.

It was not and I wanted more than anything to confide in him. But, I could not. Because of my own choices. So I just powered through the night acting fine even if I was not. I know Ray knew I was not but he did not force me to talk and I was thankful.

Comment section

WdoBest_84_ : Oh heavy and concerning you really at your breaking point.

Passeureby_102 : 🚶 You are finally facing yourself good for you and goo progress. 🚶

Seetrought93 : I am. I really needed this. I need to let it all out, because it is suffocating me.

WdoBest_84_ : I can see that. You REALLY need to let it all out. And, I am here for you I promise.

Seetrought93 : Thank you Laura.

WdoBest_84_ : Pleasure.

Seetrought93 : I think recalling that bummed me out again I am going to bed.

WdoBest_84_ : Good night.

Seetrought93 : Thanks, you too.

WdoBest_84_ : Thank you.

The Day After the Fateful Day: Fateful Day +1

A typical boring Netflix and chill solo day.

Fateful Day +2

Swimming pool early in the morning, then the same day as the day before. Still in denial about what happened on Friday. I went out to stroll around town, bought a book, took it back to read alone in my room, then when I got tired of that, I watched episodes of One Piece that I hadn't seen yet. Anyway, I did my best not to think about the beginning of my weekend, which made me go to bed late, only when I felt exhausted, knowing that I wouldn't think about anything and that I would fall directly asleep. Ray is suspicious but knows not to ask anything. When I am like this it is better to ignore me.

Fateful Day +3

Monday morning, I woke up super late, an hour late on my usual wake-up time because I clearly forgot to set the alarm the night before. So I had to hurry and run to brush my teeth, get dressed, and go to college because I was about to miss my morning class. Obviously, the hour of delay would allow me to take a shower and walk quietly to college, which was fifteen minutes on foot from my apartment, but this time I couldn't allow myself to walk, so I quickly put on my sneakers and left running, not even bothering to close the door when I noticed Ray was still there. While running, I bumped into someone, but as I was in a hurry, I just murmured a sorry without taking the time to listen to what he had to tell me, and I continued straight to my class. I arrived at the same time as the professor, and I had to hold my breath to avoid showing that I had run to get there, which tired me even more, so I sat down, breathing like a buffalo next to my friends.

- What is the matter with you? I tought you didn't know how to run ?
- Shut up and concentrate Max.
- Ok he is in a bad mood today.
- Hum.

At the end of my morning class, I was going down the stairs to exit the building when someone called me in an incongruous manner. Here are precisely the words he said to me:

- It's you, right?

At that moment, I didn't understand what he was saying nor did I realize which language he was speaking. And especially, that he was talking to me. I was standing on the landing between the second and first floor. I stood there for a moment, looking at him strangely, and so he repeated himself.

- It is you, right?
- Sorry, are you talking to me?

He smiled at me; it was a very tall young man with very black hair, very beautiful green-gray eyes, and a thin face, but still very masculine; I'll leave the rest to everyone's imagination. If one were to ask anyone, they would classify him as incredibly hot. And, for some reason that escaped me, he lived in France and spoke English with a heavy English accent. I repeated myself again since he had fallen silent and was looking at me with a mischievous smile bordering on arrogance.

–   You are obviously talking to me since we are the only ones here.

He continued his staring and then showed me my wallet in what looked like his pocket. I had no idea how he could have it since he was climbing the stairs while I was going down, and we hadn't passed each other, and he was in front of me on the second step of the stairs, so I asked him,

–   How did you find that?
–   I found it this morning and ran after you. It fell from your pocket.
–   Aww, it was you! I'm so sorry; I was late for my morning class. So that's why you have my wallet.

I don't know clearly how he managed to find me since he didn't know me at all. He later explained to me that having seen the direction I was headed, he assumed that I was going to the math faculty, so when he finished his own course that morning, he came over, and they told him to drop it off at the registry office on the third floor, and that's what he was about to do before running into me.

–   Oh, thanks very much. Can you give it back now? You don't have to go to the third floor anymore, *I told him, noticing that instead of returning it to me, he was still looking at me intently.*
–   That's you. It is really you.
–   What are you on about? Can you give my wallet back, please?
–   Hum, I will give it to you only if you tell me if it was you.

Since all this time I had primarily fixed my gaze on my wallet, I turned it toward the young man's face to examine him more thoroughly to see if I perhaps knew him. When my eyes met his, I recognized him, and I felt my heart race, and the images of that Friday night, which I had taken all my time to erase over the weekend, started to dance before my eyes. I was left hypnotized, and at the same time, I felt terrified because

I never thought I would see that person again in my life. Because I was still trying to get rid of those memories, and there they were pursuing me even more now with his presence. Upon recognizing him, I staggered back toward the stairs and bumped against the ones leading to the second floor and almost fell. He climbed the last two stairs of the first and approached me, catching me at the hips as I was losing my balance and pulled me toward him. I was so taken aback that I forgot we were communicating in English and said to him,

- Damn it, let go of me. *I said in french.*
- What did you say? *He replied to me.*
- I said stop touching me and give my fucking wallet back.
- Oh, so polite! Is this the way you usually thank people for helping you?
- I am thanking you the way I want to now. Can you stop holding me?
- Now my wallet. *I added, after he let go of me.*
- Well, for your wallet, you have to do something more. I'm not giving it back to you that easily. Now that I found you, I think it's time to talk a little bit about what happened on Friday night.
- What is it that we have to talk about? I mean, we don't know each other; that day was a horrible mistake. Here we talked about it. That was it. So, my wallet.

I could already see my patience wearing thin, and I wanted to take my wallet and go home without thinking about that fucked-up morning. But he continued to smile with that same smile while watching me lose my composure, seeming amused. I said then

- Why are you looking at me like that? What is it that I have to do for you to leave me alone after giving me my wallet?

Comment section

WdoBest_84_ : Hello, you don't write anything for months, and now you come and drop bombs on me without warning and without even saying hello first?

Seetrought93 : Sorry, I was living through crazy things that weren't nice, and I was a bit afraid to tell you and that you would insult me too much like you always do.

WdoBest_84_ : That is called tough love.

Seetrought93 : Hum.

WdoBest_84_ : Seriously, the more you fuck up, the more material I have for my book, so have fun. I'm not here to judge.

Seetrought93 : Okay, well I continue.

Passeureby_102 : 🚶 Too many bad ideas for only one person ! 🚶

Seetrought93 : I can't argue to that.

I clearly didn't know what I was getting into when I gave my number to Klaus. He was not going to stop there. He didn't just want us to be acquaintances, and obviously, you think I should have blocked him, and that's it, but no, he's much smarter than that. I still have all his messages, so let me show you.

- Hello. How are you?
- I thought I'd wait for a new day to write to you when you either forget that you gave me your number or you'd be sufficiently disappointed that I hadn't written anything (little psychological game), or maybe you blocked me which would've suited me, and I could've seen you sooner.
- In case you didn't get the hint, if you block me, I'll come see you very frequently at your faculty. And, if you think you can just avoid me, don't forget that I am very resourceful. But above all, I am rich 😊 just making myself enticing.
- So, well, since I told you he's rich, he can bribes any stupid student of my uni and get whatever he wants, personal or social information if he wanted to, so I won't be able to escape as easily as I would've liked with little work and persuation. I was well known in my faculty (not bragging). I thought it was time for me to respond to him. With the thirty messages he sent me in a week. Like
- How are you? How are things? What are you up to today? etc., blah, boring. And all of that with me not responding at any moment. So I ended up responding to find out what exactly he wanted from me.

<u>Comment section</u>

WdoBest_84_ : Still, why didn't you just block him?

Seetrought93 : Because he had already changed numbers three times when I tried besides camping in front of my building at times that was not convenient for me.

Passeureby_102 : 🚶 Insane guy alert ! 🚶

The-hot-girl_42 : enough alerts out of you danm it.

WdoBest_84_ : I told you already means and time I guess.

Seetrought93 : I see, persistent.

WdoBest_84_ : Exactly.

He proposed we meet so we could have a calm discussion. He preferred that to on the phone. So I said okay for a coffee not far from my faculty, and I was nervous and annoyed because I was wondering what I would have to do to effectively and durably get rid of him. What the hell was this discussion going to lead to? I can tell you, I was extremely apprehensive.

When I arrived, he was already settled at a table near the window, and he waved me over so I could see him and come sit across from him. He had a big smile plastered on his face. He dressed simply: black pants, white polo, and white sneakers. The whole looked quite classy on him and suited him very well. He wore a silver watch and a silver ring, also on his thumb. A navy blue jacket rested on his chair.

I sat down without returning his smile, and I simply said hello.

- Hello! You're finally here. Happy to see you too.
- Hi. Do you only use French over messages?
- Yes.
- Seriously?
- I'm kidding. It's just that I have a horrible accent when speaking French, so since I'm trying to charm you, I better not use it. And I have, if I remember correctly, one of the hottest accents, yes?

- You can stop if it's to flirt; it won't do you any good.
- Fine.
- So what do you want from me exactly?
- I just wanted to talk about that night at the club when we met. It was a hot night.
- You were not kidding; your accent is awful.
- Yeah right, funny. Stop deflecting.
- I am not.
- It was a great night, right?
- Great? Are you kidding me? Anyway, I would like to hear the rest of it.
- So yeah, it was great. And frankly, I want to replicate the experience? Your gaze never left mine from start to finish; it was amazing.
- To be completely honest, for me it is the complete opposite, I wouldn't want to remember that night ever again. I have never regretted something so much.
- Why?
- I don't have to explain myself too much.
- I don't understand you; it was one of my best experiences while clubbing, I swear.
- Whatever. Anyway, if that was all you wanted, I am going to go. Sorry, but it's not happening again.
- No, no, no. I searched for you that night without finding me, and I stumbled upon you a week later at the faculty. It's a sign. I'm not satisfied with this discussion yet.
- Fine. But, really, I don't want anything to do with you.
- Come on!
- You disappeared that night too; don't tell me you searched for me. Where did you go?
- Do you really need to ask me that? Not to waste the wonderful moment we just had, I had to take care of the huge boner you gave me with your beautiful hazel eyes. You couldn't be the only one to enjoy it.
- Ah damn. What made me ask that question, damn it. Anyway, let's drop it. I wasn't very proud afterward, which means it's not really for me, so I'll just do my best to forget, and you do what you want.
- No, I'm still not satisfied. Look, let's do it this way. I can already see you rolling your eyes, but just listen till the end, okay?
- Okay.
- Why not go on a date?
- I don't want to date.
- You promise to listen?

- Fine.
- So a simple date, you and me in one of the clubs I often frequent, and I won't ask anything. If you don't like it or want to leave, I'll do exactly what you ask without any problem. And if you hate it, I promise even while being disappointed, to leave you alone for good. And if you like it, it will be cool for both of us, don't you think?
- Hum.
- Or you can refuse, and I'll keep harassing you without scruples.
- Okay, fine, one time.
- Yes!
- And if I don't like it, you will leave me alone.
- Yes.
- You promise.
- Yes, promise. Do you want to drink something before leaving? I missed staring at you.
- No, thank you. I don't want to talk to you more than necessary. Bye.
- Your loss. I'm quite interesting. But don't worry you will find out soon enough
- I doubt it. he just responded with a smirk and weirdly enough I wanted to smile back even now I don't know exactly why but he seemed dangereuse in a way and that made me want to smile.

He gave me another big smile that I didn't return, again, and I got up and left the café as quickly as possible.

The evening of the day I spoke to him, he sent me a message in which he attached an invitation that read:

- You are invited to the erotic evening in red and black organized by Valnéria. Of course, you can come accompanied.

There was no name or address on the card, just those few words. Then I saw another message informing me that he would send me something to wear and that he would come and pick me up in person.

I was a bit impressed by all that, and above all, I felt like I was finding myself in one of those weird films that always start with a rich handsome but tortured guy who loves to torture, so I wasn't completely reassured.

<u>Comment section</u>

Seetrought93 : Yeah I said torture two times sue me. Remenber English is still not my first language.

WdoBest_84_ : I did not say a thing!

Seetrought93 : Hum! Wiered

But as he said, around 6 PM, I received a package that contained a very beautiful black suit with red silk reflections. There was a pretty red silk shirt in it too, but there was a little note advising me not to wear it because it was put there so that I could reuse the suit for other occasions than just this one.

There were also shoes and a tie that I didn't need either. I dressed up, despite my own hesitations, as he preferred, and at 8 PM sharp, he sent me a message saying he was waiting for me in front of my building.

He first took me to a chic restaurant the food was delicious I can't lie. Anyhow, I was more worried because maybe he expected me to send pictures on Instagram so that if I suddenly disappeared, they would think I was having a blast while I was being turned into a sex slave. Yes, I changed genre films. But well, as I am very much alive recounting all this, I obviously survived.

Around 9:30 PM, we left the restaurant, and he took me through dark alleys toward a sort of very dark house, which only exacerbated the fear of being kidnapped. I had absolutely no desire to get out of the car. In fact, he had to convince me by saying that my roommate knows who I am with, and he certainly didn't want to end up in prison. I wasn't sure because he was rich, but well. I had no choice; I had already gone too far.

So I got out of the car with a lot of apprehension. He took me to the black door that was in front of the brick building, which was four meters from the car, just in front of the parking lot where we parked.

Inside, there was a long dark hallway; all to make me feel even more uneasy. But at the end of the hallway, there were two guards who strangely resembled nightclub bouncers to whom Klaus showed the invitation. They let us enter the room that the hallway led to.

Inside, I found exactly what I expected, but the use was clearly contrary; I was not going to be killed. Everything in the room was either red or black. There were several different rooms, all separated by thin silk curtains. So we could see everything happening inside each of them.

A person who seemed to be a hostess of the evening handed us masks that we hurried to put on before moving deeper into the large room that seemed to be the size of a ballroom worthy of a huge castle.

In the middle of the ballroom, there was a queen-size bed on which a very erotic threesome was unfolding, which you could notice the liked the attention by the way they harmoniously undulated around each other, and the smiles and glances they threw at everyone watching them.

I turned to Klaus with a half-questioning, half-worried look and asked him what we were supposed to be doing there. I must admit I was slightly excited too. He looked at me with one of his enigmatic smiles and told me we would do exactly whatever I wanted to do. I wasn't entirely satisfied with his answer, but I didn't comment further, and we stood there for a while watching the spectacle happening before us without saying a word. Then, without me noticing, he slipped behind me, and I felt his hands first on my shoulder, then they slowly glided over my arms and then my chest. All of a sudden, I was short of breath. As I wondered what kind of movie my life had flipped into, the only answer I found at that moment was that I had gotten caught in a script worthy of a pornographic movie.

The fact is that I wasn't complaining. I let him do it was surprising me, but still I did not move a hand to stop him. Slowly and taking me by surprise, he lowered his head close to my ear: "All I'm missing now is the chance to look into your beautiful hazel eyes and see that reflection of lust that I adored last time, with that little hint of absolutely sexy mischief."

I didn't know how to respond. And his accent, which was so horrible the last time, was much more controlled. Later, he told me that he spoke to me in French because he personally found that phrases like this had the most impact in the language of the person who listened or read them.

He said : J'ai hâte de te dévergonder. Et, de te dévorer. (I can't wait to ruin you and eat you up completely)

And at that moment, I can say that personally, with that very slight hint of an English accent on top, I had an extremely hard time restraining myself upon hearing those words. I turned to him and, while plunging my gaze into his, gave him a smile mirroring the enigmatic smirk he constantly tossed at me. His smirk turn into a real smile, then pulled me closer to hims with his hands that were previously on my chest and were now on my hips. Then he kissed me first violently as if he wanted to completely draw me in. And afterward, his kisses became slower once he had assurance that I wasn't intending to escape him. Then slowly, he began depositing little kisses on my neck first, then my cheeks, my dimples; licking the hollows; my chin, then again my dimples, my right ear, then the left, and he whispered in the hollow of my ear:

- You have no idea of the effect you have on me right now. I have an extreme urge to take you right here in front of all these people and give them a second performance even more exciting than the first.

At that moment, I was already trembling with excitement, but the words he pronounced so close to my ears made me lose my footing. He continued :

- Just look to your left; there's a young redhead with green eyes who is watching us intently. Do you feel like inviting him to join us in a room for a little game?
- I turned and saw the guy in question who gave me a wide smile followed by a wink. I nodded and lowered my eyes before hesitantly saying, Do you want him to watch us, or is it you who wanting to watch him with me?
- Both. Wait for me here; I'm going to talk to him."

I nodded. What the hell was I doing ? It sounds like an excuse but the mask was kind of making me feel free.

I saw him head toward the young man in question. They chatted for two or three minutes, smiling mischievously and looking directly at each other. It was clear they were flirting, but that word wasn't enough to precisely describe what I was witnessing. They seemed extremely intimate and sexual just using their looks and words. After a moment that I found too short, I was not sure to be ready, yet. They came toward me, and without a word, klaus took my hand, and we went straight toward one of the small rooms separated from one another only by thin, translucent silk curtains.

In there, Klaus sat in a corner while Caleb, as the redhead introduced himself later, came toward me with dark eyes full of desire. I sat on the bed and watched him approach. He didn't try even once, to kiss me on the lips, and got immediately down to business which I found strange at first but which I liked a lot. Later, Klaus told me he had asked him not when they conversed at the beginning. While throughout that time Caled and I were on the bed, Klaus never took his gaze from me, and every time my gaze wandered off him, he came back to turn my gaze toward him, by proding my chin up or by making a little noise to make his presence awared of. He would also come kiss me, and then returned to his previous position.

When Caleb approached me, he first took off the top of my jacket and kissed my neck, then my chest, teasing my nipple before moving down toward my pants. Now, he knelt in front of me, took off my pants, and started massaging my balls before taking me into his mouth.

After a while, Klaus approached again. Our gazes had not left each other, and he leaned toward me, kissed me passionately before pushing Caleb away and taking his place. He took me into his mouth too with avidity, with his gaze still locked on mine. Then afterward, he placed several small kisses on my belly before standing up and taking off his clothes. He gently pushed me down to lay me on the bed, then he hovered above me and kissed me again for a moment I had closed my eyes but when I opended them I realised by his look that he never closed his. So I found myself trappes once again into his greedy look. As if he wanted to watch into my soul. The only moments when we didn't look into each other's eyes was when he kissed me, because I always closed my eyes. I had no idea when he had put on the condom, but the fact that he took me while not taking his gaze away from mine made me realize he had much more experience than I thought. And when he saw that I was about to growl (grunt) loudly, he muffled it with a long kiss. I was breathless; however, I noticed, in my peripheral vision, that Caleb had started to touch himself while looking at us.

At around 5 AM, Klaus was dropping me off in front of my building. I hadn't opened my mouth during the trip. I was a little shy at the moment. Once again what the hell was I thinking behaving in such a way ? He had offered to take me to his place because it was closer, but I didn't want to. I needed to find myself in a familiar environment in order to think things through and try to better understand what had just happened to me.

The first thing I did when I got home was to take a long shower. I completely didn't care what time it was and that I risked waking Ray up. I needed to get rid of any trace of lust from my body. I had no idea what to think; I was completely disturbed by what I had had the courage to do.

After the shower, I went straight into the kitchen. I made myself a huge sandwich with a ton of melted cheese, then I went back to my room, turned on my computer, and started watching a cartoon as if I were a kid who had just watched a horror movie. As you could guess, I'm a little of a stress eater.

Anyway, instead of doing what I initially wanted to do, reflecting on my screw-up, I did everything to not even think about my evening. Very good idea to run away from your problems; you'll see that later, it worked out for me immensely. In any case, the fact is that I fell asleep in front of my cartoon and didn't wake up until Ray started knocking on my door. I looked at the time: it was 1 PM. I had certainly recovered well. I rubbed my eyes, stretched, and then got up to go open the door for him.

- What time did you get back last night?
- Hello to you too.
- So?
- I got back around 5 in the morning.
- That's what I thought. Where were you?
- Out with a friend.
- Which one?
- You don't know him.
- Even better. And, your phone wasn't working?
- It was, but I didn't think I'd take that long, and at that moment I completely forgot to let you know.
- I noticed. Plus, you posted a few photos on Instagram at the beginning of the evening, and then radio silence. Not very reasuring.
- I'm sorry; yesterday you told me you were going to see your cousins and your uncle and that afterward, you might return the next day, so I didn't really think to let you know, especially since I thought I'd come back early.
- I see; you must have been surprised to see my keys in the entry when you got back.
- Yeah, clearly.
- Hum. And for you, that gives you an excuse to not tell me you were going out. This way, if there's a problem, I just have to say I wasn't supposed to be there, so I have nothing to say. That's how it always works.
- No, no, that's really not what I meant.
- So?
- I'm sorry.

- Yeah. Anyway, did you sleep well?
- Yeah, thanks. And you?
- I have no complaints.

Only at that moment did he leave my bedroom entrance to head back toward the living room. I put on a t-shirt and went out to join him.

- So, was it good with your uncle yesterday?
- Yeah, for the most part. You know he doesn't pretend when it comes to hosting. Even for a small birthday party, he hired the best caterer. But, like always, there was bound to be a topic of discord between him and one of his children.
- And what was the subject of the dispute this time?
- His daughter was telling me and her brothers about a girl in her project group who had tried to flirt with her. He passed by just as she was saying that the girl told her she dressed super sexy, and he flipped his lid. Said it wasn't a proper girl to be conversing with, and she shouldn't ever receive her again, and he wouldn't tolerate that nonsense in his house.
- Then it went off into counternature, etc.
- Exactly.
- He's had that kind of discussion with my mom while watching an episode of Four Weddings and a Honeymoon in which there was a gay couple.
- Hum, typical. By the way, he asked why you didn't come, and I told him you had a lot of work right now. He's a little mad at you for missing his birthday, but he wishes you good luck for your studies.
- Thank you very much. I'm sure you,, stayed quiet in your corner through out the whole discussion.
- Exactly. I don't have any desire to debate that with him. My parents know I am pan; the rest can just mind their own business.
- Totally right.
- Hum. So do you want breakfast? Anything in particular? I'm going to take out the trash and then do some shopping.
- It's 1 PM; it's no longer breakfast.
- I admit I didn't wake up early either, so it's breakfast for you like me, or if you want, brunch. So?
- Whatever you want, Ray.
- Okay. Bacon, eggs, milk, orange juice, and/or mixed fruits, assorted croissants and bread with butter.

- We're having how many people exactly?
- No one.
- So all of this is for why?
- So you have plenty of choice and can't complain afterward about not liking anything.
- I never do that.
- Hum. Anyway, you'll eat hardly anything, and I'll eat almost everything in two days. Perfect.
- Rather say you're extremely hungry.
- Anyway, a brunch is made to have an abundance of choice. And, by the way, I nearly forgot the fruits.
- Grapes, tangerines, apples, peaches, strawberries.
- Are you sure the peach is in season?
- We'll see.
- Well, go, and make sure not to raid the store.
- Whatever. Anyway, we'll be too lazy to go out tomorrow morning, so it's perfect.
- At this rate, we might even be able to get through the whole coming week in terms of breakfast.
- Nothing to complain about.
- Totally agree.

He put on his sneakers, took the trash out, and left. Unlike me, he was decently dressed. While waiting for him to bring back breakfast, I brushed my teeth and was finishing up my shower when he came back. He yelled to me,

- You're in luck; I ran into your delivery guy when I got back, or else he would have gone to the relay or back to the post office
- What are you talking about? I'm not expecting any delivery.
- I came out of the shower with a towel around my waist.
- Stop splashing water everywhere; dry yourself properly before coming out.
- It's fine; I didn't make but two drops, let me be. Did you by chance get the wrong name? I didn't order anything at all.
- You are William K. Smith, right?
- Um, yes.
- Well, I'm leaving the package on the couch.
- Okay. It's still weird; I have no idea what it can be."

I cleaned myself better, went to dress in my room, and came out to see what was in the package. It was a medium-sized box, about 30 cm by 24 cm. I took a knife and began to open it. Inside, I found a smaller case that contained a red jockstrap with a note that read, "It was a pleasure last night, and I hope we'll do it more often." I was so surprised that I jumped when I heard Ray speak behind me. He had changed in his room to wear more comfortable clothes. He had exchanged his shirt and jeans for a t-shirt and shorts. When I turned around, he had an inquisitive look fixed on me.

- So?
- Pardon? I didn't hear what you said.
- I see that. I was asking what that was, and if you had finally remembered when you ordered it.
- Ah, uh, yes, yes, of course! What a fool I am. Actually, it's a razor that my mom and I bought for my dad.
- Ah, that's right; his birthday is coming up. I should look for something to give him too. By the way, can you show it to me?
- Uh, no, I don't like this one; I'm going to return it and get another one. It doesn't match the photo on the site at all.
- Show me anyway.
- No, *I said.* Well, I'll put it away in my room for now.
- You're acting weird all of a sudden.
- Not at all.
- So then what's going on?
- I'm just saying that I'm feeling interrogated here.
- Very well, if that's how you're taking it.
- Exactly. Go cook already.

He kept looking at me suspiciously. I wen into my room keeping the package behind me closed of course. went I was out of Ray's gaze I put on my desk and headed out making sure to close my door properly behind me taking my phone with me.

- So what are we making first ?
- The bacon and the eggs I gess.
- Let's do it.
- So you are not telling me what was actually in the box really ?
- Not now maybe later.
- Ok

So we started cooking our late brunch. During that time I was just following his orders about the cookin. Afterward we put everything on the table to start eating. We were both on our phones so noone was talking. It was a little weird. It was the first time that I was keeping something from him. I mean apart from you know what. I was just too ashamed to tell him anything. So, I just kept quiet.

Afterward I went back to my room to call Klaus.

- I just received you package. You could have told me, what if Ray opened it ?
- What is a Ray.
- Rude ! He is my roommate.
- It's a guy ?
- yeah !
- Your boyfriend or something ?
- No !
- So then what is the matter ?
- What ?
- You did not even ask if I was alright, if I slept well and directly started nagging at me because that Ray person could have seen something he actually did not.
- Are you kidding me ?
- I think that Ray guy's opinion is too important for you and I don't like it.
- What ? No but he is a childhood friend, our parents are friends and all that. You know ?
- Ok if you say so.
- No but did the roles reverse ? I was complaining about you buying stupid stuff for me.
- you don't like it?
- No.
- Really ? It is for the next time we see each other.
- Well, there would not be another time. what made you think there would be another ?
- Your moaning yesterday.
- Well, there won't be a next time.
- You sure about that? Now that you've had a taste, you won't be able to live without it.
- What about your cock?

- I was talking about the sensations, but that too. I'll admit I've got a good loinset. And then my accent speaking French you must have really lost your head.
- Are you making fun of me?
- Not at all
- You know I'm tired, I'll leave you to it.
- I know yesterday was really tiring. I'll give you that. I'm surprised you're even up. But I guess you must have been hungry.
- Urgh... Whatever
- Go get some rest I'm going to go organize our next outing.
- I already said there won`t be one.
- Right.

The rest of the weekend was quiet. I went out a bit with my mates and Ray and tried to ignore Klaus.

But of course I couldn't keep ignoring him, which didn't stop me from trying. On Monday, when I arrived in front of my college, he was waiting for me with coffee and croissants.

- I hope you're hungry, *he said, moving away from the wall he was leaning against. He handed me the coffee.*
- I don't drink coffee.
- Chocolate then? *He hands me the second glass.*
- I don't want any.
- Are you sure? I went to a lot of trouble.
- Back to French?
- I'm trying, aren't I?
- Hmm. I've got class.
- You're 30 minutes early, can't we have lunch? Don't be so cold or I'll feel used.
- Fine.

So we entered the buildings. There was a lunch/review area on the 4th floor with computers and other devices to recharge, so that's where we went to settle down. We sat down face to face. I ended up taking the hot chocolate and a croissant.

- So how do you like it?
- It's pretty basic, I don't see what there is to criticize.

- You're absolutely right. Tell me, why did you take the trouble to ignore me this weekend?
- Because I felt like it.
- I see.
- What about now?
- Like what?
- Do you still feel like it?
- Yes, but I don't suppose you're going to let me.
- Well, I'm not going to let you.
- Wasn't the deal that you'd leave me alone after Friday?
- No. The deal was that you'd stop running away from me after you realized how good I am in bed.
- Ah!
- No, but more seriously, you didn't seem disappointed on Friday, so I thought we were past that stage of, "this isn't like me, I don't want to do this bullshit again". How much longer are you going to keep lying to yourself?
- I'm not lying to you. I'm really not interested in you. And I really don't like the urges I get when I'm with you.
- Tell me about those urges.
- No but that's enough you're really too full of yourself.
- I just know what I am worth.
- Hum.
- So what are your concerns this time around that we're talking about it because normally we'd say if you don't like it you leave but you liked it and you still want to go?
- Yes. It's precisely because I liked it that I want to leave.
- Well, I refuse and I want to talk about it together.
- Talk about what exactly?
- What you're afraid of.
- I'm not afraid of anything.
- Will?
- Fine. I don't want to make what happened on Friday a habit.
- I promise it won't.
- Fine. But what else are you doing?
- I'm gonna go watch strangers fuck in nightclubs.
- Go fuck yourself.

- Just kidding, it's fine.
- Hum.
- So I go out with my buddies and we eat and drink like everybody else.
- You're telling me.
- In fact, we're going out for a drink on Wednesday night, do you want to come and meet them?
- I'll let you know if I can tonight.
- You always have to think about everything, don't you?
- Well, yes.
- I'm beginning to understand you, so I'll be going. You should go to class.
- Yes, I'm going.

For the rest of the day I heard nothing from Klaus, and even that evening he didn't ask me what I'd decided. I wondered if he was busy and what he was busy with. I told myself I wouldn't write to him either until he asked me if I was coming with him. But I had to admit I missed him a bit with his incessant messages and salacious comments. I didn't hear from him the next day either, so I decided to write that I couldn't join him the next evening with his mates. I expected him to pester me to change my mind, but he didn't. He didn't reply until three o'clock in the afternoon. He didn't reply until 3 p.m. that day and, as if to surprise me even more, he said it didn't matter and that he'd see me another day. I admit I was disappointed and wondered what I'd said or done that had turned him off so much.

Later that evening I wrote to tell him that I could go after all, and that my bogus excuse had been cancelled. He seemed pleased enough to reassure me, and so he told me he'd come and pick me up at my place again, which he did. On Wednesday, he picked me up to go to a bar in the 1st arrondissement of Paris. When we arrived, his buddies were already there. There were five of them. We sat around a round table and, starting from my left, there were Quentin, Loïc, Édouard, Mike and Henri. Klaus introduced me to the whole table and they greeted me warmly. They all seemed nice, but the one I got on with the most was Mike.

Was he less wealthy and therefore me full of himself? Absolutely, and as a result there were certain jokes that only the two of us understood, which helped us connect more quickly. What's more, he was happy to make fun of his mates with me, which was great because they were almost all stuck up their arses on different scales. The evening went quite well, we all had more than one go at it, and it loosened tongues beautifully.

I had a class in the afternoon, so I couldn't go home, and we'd both finished, so we went into a Monoprix to see what we could buy. We soon realized we could only get one or two oranges. I won't say how much we had. Anyway, when we were weighing our oranges, a group of girls came by and started talking about how many pizzas they were going to buy for the evening and what they were going to go with them. We found ourselves bursting out laughing without really knowing why. It took us a long time to get our act together. We grabbed our oranges and walked out of the monoprix completely hilarious.

Mike immediately burst out laughing while the others looked at us as if we'd lost our minds. I was laughing too, but I stopped to ask them why they were staring at us like that.

- What, you don't think it's funny?
- Of course they don't understand, it's something that can never happen to them.
- Yes, I don't understand at all, *says Quentin.*
- You're perhaps the most uptight of all, aren't you? *replies Mike.*
- Please don't do that again.
- Well, it's a pity you don't understand anything, but it's extremely funny.
- Well, it's late, so I guess you'll be going home since you've got school in the morning.
- Yes, thanks.

We parted on that note. On the way home, I asked Klaus why all evening Quentin seemed to resent Mike's existence, and he replied that he'd never understood how their relationship worked. It really was a lovely evening and I had more fun than I thought I would, and I remarked to Klaus when he pulled up in front of my building. He gave me a big smile as he kissed me languorously before stepping out to open the door for me to leave.

- What gallantry, I'm not a young lady you need to impress.
- No, you're a young man I want in my bed.
- You can't hold back any longer from talking nonsense, can you?
- No, I couldn't.
- Mmm.
- Well, are you sure you don't want to sleep at my place? I will take care of you affectionately, and I'm also very close to the faculty.
- No thanks.

- Good night, dear.
- Night.
- Don't dream too much about me. You'll be really tired afterward.
- Fuck off.

And it was on those words that he left. When I was about to close the gate behind me, I heard someone tell me to hold the door. I recognized the voice; it was Ray. He looked slightly annoyed. I let him in, then turned with the gate shut to give one last wave to Klaus, who returned it before driving away. Then I turned to Ray.

- So who was it? *He had a questioning look.*
- Um, it's a friend, a new friend.
- Do all your friends shove their tongues down your throat?
- Um, it might be a bit more than a friend ?
- Maybe?
- Is the interrogation over already ? I'd like to go rest rather than discuss downstairs all night.
- Very well, if that's how you treat me.
- Exactly. Good night.

I went to the elevator without waiting for his response. He closely followed me but didn't say a word. I was grateful for that. We didn't talk about the evening. I took a shower and went to bed. The next day wasn't brighter either. When I woke up, I had breakfast at the dining table just in front of his room. When he got up too, he didn't say a word to me. He barely greeted me. He took an expeditious shower, got ready, and left. I hardly ever argued with Ray, or rather never, and moreover, he was very calm and rather direct, so he didn't speak unless he had something to say, and most importantly, he didn't ignore me without a reason. That's why I felt hurt and worried when he ignored me without even giving me a glance. I just decided I would leave him alone for the day and talk to him later in the evening to see where he stood and especially about the bullshit I had said the day before.

That evening there was a small argument, but it was fixed over time. Plus, I always highlighted Ray's direct side.

When night fell, my plan was thus to get closer to him and, um, to tell him that I was sorry for the nonsense I said to him, that I had never told him I was bi even though

I knew it, that I had never completely been honest regarding what was happening, and, um, to explain to him without really telling him the truth (like I was still a little ashamed of the first night) how Klaus and I met. That we were just in a bar, that we clicked instinctively, that we talked a lot, exchanged numbers, and that was it. I didn't go into details of the encounter. I felt there was a bit of disappointment in his gaze, about the fact I had never been honest with him already, that I felt the need to hide it so long. As if I wasn't trusting enough of him or that I thought he'd be disappointed in me, which couldn't be the case at all. So from that moment on, we started to talk to each other again, half as before, but I still felt a distance between him and me, and I knew it wasn't me who was at fault. I could not really blame him because it was not him who had done wrong. I had pushed him to distance himself, and he had only followed the path I had laid out for us.

On the other hand, after a week or two, I thought it had to be good for us, for him, that he finally meets Klaus, and I had the idea to organize a dinner in our apartment and invited Klaus to join us and enter for the first time into the apartment. We went straight to the table, without an appetizer. I had never experienced an atmosphere as heavy and silent as this one. Ray, who was already normally taciturn and calm, was even more so, and he was exceptionally cold, only responding in monosyllables.

Like for instant.

-   What's your name again?
-   Ray.
-   What are you studying?
-   I am in business school.
-   Where are you from?
-   Bordeaux, etc...

And so on and so forth. In short, there was no enthusiasm or a hint of an "And you?" So there was no interest. I was starting to get a headache.

It felt like I was a teacher who had punished two rival students by forcing them to be in the same room and to be courteous to each other. Because I never saw a hint of a smile on the faces of my two prisoners or the a shadow of interest in each other. So it was an extremely cold dinner, and I didn't know where to put myself. I thought that from then on I wouldn't force them to be together, especially not alone because I risked having the worst evening of my life. They was determined not to get along, and I didn't completely understand why.

I later noticed that Klaus didn't see things favorably whenever I talked about Ray. And one day, while we had just dined together and were in his apartment watching a movie, right in the middle of the film (while two protagonists were arguing in the film about a jealousy issue from one), suddenly he turned to me and you won't guess what he said to me.

- Yes?
- Um, did you and Ray not have a little thing, an experiment or something like that?
- Ugh what did you say?
- Well, nothing; I don't know he is kind of hot and you seem to get along pretty well
- Yeah ! He is my best friend it is normal to get along. Ray and I don't see each other like that.
- Hum.
- What?
- It's true that you're so close, it's a bit hard not to be jealous.
- Bullshit. With all the thing we do together you know how to get jealous ?
- It is not the same. I am always there and I limited their access to you. They are just tools for us to have fun together.
- Ok but you don't have anything to be jalous of when it come to Ray.
- If you say so.
- I do. And I was not realizing we were that serious.
- Well I am.
- I can see that.
- I had hoped you would be too.
- I guess I am getting there too. *He kissed me and then hugged me from behind and made me lean Completely on him instead of the couch and we concentrated once more on the movie.*

Anyway, from that moment on, he became much more paranoid. He started asking me to move in with him or at least to move out of Ray's place. And above all, he had absolutely no intention of making an effort to get closer to Ray because he had the impression that our relationship was too fusion-like, as you just said. So we had a lot of fierce arguments on the subject; I tried to make him understand that Ray was my best friend, that he was one of the persons who mattered the most in my life and that it was absolutely impossible for me to stop seeing him much less stop living with him for the moment because I loved being with him. So there was really no chance that I'd stop seeing him.

I knew that these facts were truly hard to accept for Klaus, but he began to understand that he didn't really have a choice. He talked to me a lot about it often. On the other hand, Ray and I were still a bit distant. And, I couldn't really talk to him about Klaus because he didn't like him as well. So now what I do is that I separate them completely. On one side I have Ray, and on the other, I have Klaus, and I don't talk about one with the other and especially do not make them see each other.

On the other hand, Klaus no longer suggested to do fun things like the night I feared getting killed as often. I would say it was getting less and less about those gathering and more about just the both of us. So at the moment, I didn't mention it to Klaus, and I let myself get immersed in the relationship, but little by little, I think I began to feel a lack regarding this kind of situation. I was developing cravings for intense experiences, of the sort. I suppose, but above all, now that I think about it, I just wanted to be seen more, that is why it started with him anyway. So I asked him when he would make me relive that kind of experience. And he was surprised, or rather I'm sure he was feigning surprise, but well. He told me,

- I thought that's what almost made me lose you in the beginning.
- No, not at all. I found it fun, and I want to try it again. To understand a bit why I loved or rather liked it so much. Especially now that everything is going well between us.
- Ok, let's do that tomorrow night.
- In fact, you were just waiting for me to ask.
- Touché, well, I thought that when you were interested, you would tell me, and it would come from you, and you wouldn't be able to blame me for it. This way, we both know you're interested too.
- You sick asshole.
- Love you too. I know you like my sadistic ways.So tomorrow night, I'll dress you up again.
- Ok.
- And for the underwear, you can use my gift.
- I forgot about that.
- How could you?

- I made myself forget. Ray was the one to get the package downstairs and I had to lie to him.
- Ray hum ? It seems lying to him is too grave. come on it is not that big of a deal.
- You know what just forget what i just said.
- Hum Anyway I would like to see you in those.

The next day, I was excited all day for the evening. Another place, same kind of decoration, all in white. Everyone was masked, women and men alike. This time he seemed to have planned everything and took me directly to a room all the way at the back left, a little more hidden, and inside awaited us seems a young girl and two guys. And even in this situation, I noticed that he generally remained possessive over me and didn't allow me to have sex with anyone else but him. He was really against it, and when I nearly went through with it, he immediately pulled me away. The others watched us more than they participated. After that night, we started doing a lot more of those kinds of things, and I ended up realizing that what I really enjoyed in all of this was just being seen by other people as bisexual. And being accepted in a welcoming environment. And it was becoming some sort of obsession I was getting addicted to the sensations I got from being watched without realizing it. It was having négative impacts on my studies but I couldn't care less. I was craving it and I was done depriving myself.

We even started bringing people from different bars home, be it to his or rarely to mine when I was closer and when I had classes or when Ray was not present. I did it less often since he seemed to strongly disapprove. I only really went home when I couldn't do otherwise or when he wasn't there. Especially at that moment. These weren't situations that would improve our relationship, Ray and I, especially after saying that he recognized me less and less as being the person he had known for more than ten years. Especially since he had an idea of what I was doing and I knew he found it not very mature or whatever by his standards. But I don't know why I still wanted him to know the person I was becoming. I don't know if I'm clear enough. He meant a lot to me. I needed hiem to know me still.

On the other hand, regarding my studies, my grades had suffered due to my constant outings with Klaus, and I felt I no longer saw anyone other than him, and that our relationship was increasingly revolving around sex and nothing else. So, as my environment was almost entirely limited to my relationship with Klaus and therefore an unhealthy relationship with my sexuality just for the purpose of feeling seen. And I was increasingly realizing this, but I didn't really want to accept it because otherwise it would mean having to give it up and I really did not want to.

One day I clearly overstepped boundaries because I had a heated argument with Ray, who was no longer discussing with me; but there you go. It was the day after a night spent with Klaus, from which I'd come home super late. I had chosen to skip my classes, and I woke up late to have breakfast. Ray was having breakfast, so I greeted him.

– Hello, how are you? Sleep well?

He didn't answer me, so I thought he hadn't heard, and I approached him and attempted to wave my right hand in front of his eyes. He turned toward me and told me :

– What are you doing?
– I'm greeting you; clearly, you're in a daze and didn't hear me?
– I mean, what are you becoming? What are you doing with your life?
– Nothing. I don't understand your question.
– You left your model on the table yesterday. I see you're still not holding up in your studies.
– I know it's not great, but that's none of your business. I'll manage, don't worry.
– Don't worry? While you're messing up your life with the idiot you've chosen as your boyfriend?
– I forbid you to speak about him like that.
– You're not forbidding me anything; I do what I want as long as we live together, I feel responsible for seeing you fall for such a big jerk.
– No, but what's got into you all of a sudden?
– Maybe I'm tired of watching my best friend behave like a low-level prostitute. Or rather a nympho; I don't know.
– Klaus is right; I should move out.
– No, it's me who's leaving. I don't want to see you turn into an idiot.
– I forbid you to talk to me like this. *We had begun to raise our voices.* And since when are you giving me lessons on morality? I'm not forcing you to follow me or anything, so get off your high horse. You're nobody to speak to me this way.
– Yes, indeed, I'm nobody. That's what I notice.
– That's not what I meant to say. You're my best friend...
– No, you're right; I should go to my uncle's and then organize my move; it would be for the best.

- No, I...
- Yes, I'm tired of watching you destroy yourself, and you won't have to put up with my moral lessons anymore.
- But no, don't leave.
- Yes, I'm tired. I'm going.

That afternoon, I went to see Klaus to tell him everything and receive a little comfort because I was lost, but all we did was have sex again. When I came home, Ray was no longer there; he had moved out, and he left me a message telling me not to contact him, that he was going to stay at his uncle's for good and would send people to collect his things when he found a new apartment.

I was even more devastated, and the only two people I would have wanted to talk to, I couldn't. Ray because he hated me and my mom because I would have to lie about several details, and I saw no point in it. Moreover, Klaus did not understand my distress, especially when I recounted our discussion more clearly, and he seemed extremely pleased with how things were turning out. And told me that even if Ray spoke to me again, to block him and not to approach him anymore. He even asked me to move in with him again, which I refused. We had another violent argument, and I made it clear to him that Ray meant more to me than him, and if he asked me to choose, I would choose Ray (which he did).

I came home and spent the rest of the week locked up in my place brooding and stuffing my face like a pig. I was still freed from Klaus, which allowed me to refocus on myself. I ended up fully diving back into my studies the following week, at least to tell myself that I hadn't wasted my entire life. Even though I struggled not to call Klaus when Ray completely ignored me, but I deleted his number and forced myself to concentrate on my studies and nothing else; but above all to start seeing Dr. Parker more regularly because I really wasn't doing well. She therefore wrote to me everything I was thinking and everything that happened to me in a sort of journal to regain clarity and figure out what I wanted.

<u>Comment section</u>

WdoBest_84_ : Okay, okay, all this is fine, but you didn't tell me about the breakup with Klaus clearly enough. Tell me everything clearly.

Passeureby_102 : 🚶 **Sonething smells fishy !** 🚶

The-hot-girl_42 : I have to agree with the insane guy.

Seetrought93 : Am I forced to ?

WdoBest_84_ : Yes, I think it will help you feel better.

Seetrought93 : I'm not so sure.

WdoBest_84_ : Expelling is always good.

Seetrought93 : Okay. You are just being nosy but alright.

So, as I told you, I went to see him right after Ray left and told him everything about the fight, omitting details that could make him too violent.

- What do you think I said that could make him angry?
- Just trust me.
- If you say so.
- Can I continue?
- Yes, of course.
- So I told him, and when I finished, instead of taking me in his arms to reassure me, he smiled;
- Why are you smiling?
- Sorry, it's just that I'm relieved you finally got rid of him.
- How?
- Well, yeah, I think your relationship is really toxic.
- Toxic?
- I'd even say unhealthy.
- Where are you getting these big words all of a sudden?
- I know how to speak French; I just have a horrible accent.
- Then stop talking because you're saying nonsense. Don't talk about him that way; I do not at all want to get rid of him. Never.
- I understand that it's hard to accept; it's for the best.
- Stop talking, I'm telling you.
- Okay, I'll stop.

- He's not out of my life for good; I'm sure of it.
- Come here, *he told me, pulling me into his arms. He wrapped his arms around me, and we stayed there for a while. Then he asked if I wanted something to eat.*
- I'm not hungry, thanks. I just want to stay here and do nothing for a while.
- Or I can make you feel better.
- I don't think it's the right time.
- I'll just give you a massage, don't worry.

This is exactly what he did at first, then little by little, he began giving me gentle kisses on the shoulders, and then it quickly escalated, as you can imagine.

When we finished, we fell asleep, but I woke up 20 minutes later with a startle without knowing exactly why. Then I realized how stupid I had been to come here for comfort, and Ray's words echoed in my head. I hurried to get dressed with a feeling of shame that I couldn't shake out of my head. He finally woke up with the noise I was making, and he looked at me, first surprised, and then he sat up and turned toward me.

- What are you doing?
- I'm leaving.
- Why?
- I never want to see you again.
- What are you talking about?
- I'm saying I never want to see you again. I'm breaking up with you, and I'm going home.
- How are you breaking up?
- I made a mistake by coming here.
- No, not at all. You didn't make a mistake. I'm here for you; what's wrong all of a sudden?

At this point, he had gotten up and grabbed my shoulders. I jumped at the contact as if I had received a shock. I saw in his gaze that he felt lost and hurt by my reaction.

- Don't touch me.
- Why?
- I just don't want to; I want to go home. *I had finished getting dressed and was about to grab my bag to leave when he ripped it from my hands, threw it on the floor, and held my wrists in his hands.*

- What are you doing?
- You're not going anywhere. Clearly not to see that asshole.
- You can't hold me here. *I violently withdrew, but this made him lose his balance, and I took the opportunity to grab my bag and head towards the exit.*
- You're mine.
- I'm really not.
- You are! *He had stood up and was right behind me. He tried to grab me, but I kicked him in the groin and bolted out.*
- I'm cutting ties for good. *I yelled at him.*

I threw him the keys to his apartment, and I slammed the door.

He stills tries to contact me to this day but I am doing my best ignoring him. Even if he is extremely persistent as you can imagine.

<u>**Comment section**</u>

WdoBest_84_ : Real sassy bottom.

Seetrought93 : That's not funny.

WdoBest_84_ : I was trying to cheer you up. Lighten the mood.

Seetrought93 : I know, but stop. And I'm not a sassy bottom.

WdoBest_84_ : Really?

Seetrought93 : Yes, but you know?

WdoBest_84_ : Sorry.

Seetrought93 : Well, that's what happened that day.

WdoBest_84_ : And what parts of the argument didn't you tell Klaus because I assume you didn't tell me either. Since I can't figure out what in what you said could annoy him more.

Seetrought93 : There is nothing more. Drop it.

WdoBest_84_ : I want to know.

Seetrought93 : I said to drop it.

Passeureby_102 : 🚶 fishier 🚶

WdoBest_84_ : Okay, if you insist. But I'm always here if you want to talk to me later.

Seetrought93 : Thank you; that's what a diary is for.

WdoBest_84_ : Ugh

Seetrought93 : That's usually my line.

WdoBest_84_ : I know.

PART 3

Now that I think about it, I realize what an idiot I've been. With my sessions with the psychiatrist to get me out of my black hole, reconsidering all the events of the last two years, I decided to return to Bordeaux with my family to celebrate Christmas and New Year's in familiar surroundings to try to forget my worries a little and refocus.

But on the way home I realized something that gave me a rude awakening to what I'd always had inside me that was screwing up my life. My desire never to disappoint my family meant that I had no way of explaining why I wasn't feeling well or even confiding in them. But also, I had no one to confide in, and the week that was supposed to make me feel better was just going to make me feel lonelier. And make me feel even more desperate to see him. I felt myself wasting all my energy thinking about how I couldn't explain Ray's absence and still act as if nothing had happened.

And so I arrived in a festive atmosphere with people around me, my family, and I felt more alone than I had ever felt since my father died. I had to act like I was happy and well when I wasn't and lie about Ray and act like everything was perfect. I was lonely. I was drained of all my energy and I couldn't show it or vent. My mother seemed worried but I could only tell her that everything was fine and that I was just tired from studying. I had to make more and more effort to get involved in family activities ....

He was right next door, but I'd never felt him so far away. They chatted and I quickly left the room on one pretext or another. And I've never felt so bad, so disgusted, embarrassed, disappointed, ashamed, but above all craving just to be with him; to talk to him, to see him, to feel him, to be close to him. I even felt downright jealous of my mother because she was able to talk to him, hold his hand and look at him kindly, wishing him all the best. Above all, to be able to receive his smile. I felt like I'd lost my breath of life.

I realized that the day I had decided that he should be part of my life, I hadn't done it because I wanted a best friend, but because I already had feelings for him. And I told myself that I wanted to be friends with him because even then I was lying to myself, and only now did I realize how dishonest I could be with my own feelings. And with this behavior I had lost one of the most beautiful relationships, if not the most beautiful, of my life. So I clearly had the worst vacation possible and I came back from vacation clearly sadder but also more determined to do anything to get him back even if it turned out to be true for more than one reason.

<u>Comment Section</u>

WdoBest_84_ : I've just seen what you've been writing over the vacations and I can see you've been having some serious fun.

Seetrought93 : Did you see that ?

WdoBest_84_ : Yes, yes, I almost envy you.

Seetrought93 : We can swap if you like.

WdoBest_84_ : I said almost. Take it easy.

Seetrought93 : Okay. Your lost.

WdoBest_84_ : Honestly, how did you feel when you saw him again?

Seetrought93 : I died and came back to life.

WdoBest_84_ : Stop it. You're overreacting.

Seetrought93 : Yeah, I know, but for the moment, that's what it felt like.

WdoBest_84_ : Wow.

Seetrought93 : And I was so mad at him too. How can he show up in front of me like that without embarrassment when we haven't spoken in so long and just ignore me.

WdoBest_84_ : From what I understand, you're the one who left.

Seetrought93 : Yes, but no, he came over and gave me a quick hello without really looking at me, and then he went off to give my mother some flowers and fruit, smiling at her as if nothing had happened, all pleased with himself, so I left so as not to disturb them too much, if you know what I mean.

WdoBest_84_ : I think it was an excuse to see you.

Seetrought93 : Did not feel like it.

WdoBest_84_ : And, you ran away with your tail between your legs as usual because you couldn't really bear to see him without being able to do anything to improve your present situation.

Seetrought93 : Who's side are you on?

WdoBest_84_ : The truth.

Seetrought93 : You're not really here for this, you must be on my side.

WdoBest_84_ : No, that's just it. I have to be neutral to help you better, I think.

Seetrought93 : Right.

WdoBest_84_ : So what are you going to do?

Seetrought93 : I still don't know.

WdoBest_84_ : Ugh

WdoBest_84_ : By the way, I think if Ray came to say hi to your mom just to see you. He's got it bad for you.

Seetrought93 : You think!

WdoBest_84_ : And I'm sure he did.

Passeureby_102 : 🚶 The guy is begging to hear an apology to come to you god open your fucking eyes. 🚶

Two Weeks Later

So, being alone in his apartment, with no one to talk to, having nothing to do but reflect on what I've done and what my life has become, made me remember our meeting, mine and Ray's, in sixth grade. I had just changed schools between kindergarten and middle school, and I didn't know many people like most people when entering middle school, except for those who came in groups because they were from the same primary school or whatever. And I did know others, but none very close, except for Liam. And for me, he was the only one who was still what you'd call a true friend, and he was in that middle school with me.

<u>Comment section</u>

WdoBest_84_ : Hold on; you're going to tell me about your meeting and all that now?

Seetrought93 : That's what I'm going to talk about with Doctor Parker next week, so I'm preparing. And you're not choosing the topics. I'm even sure you'll like it.

WdoBest_84_ : I'll shut up because you're right; it's not really up to me to choose. But now that you say it will interest me, I'm a little more scared.

Seetrought93 : Well, here I go.

So, in sixth grade, I didn't talk much with others, and I often liked to read in my corner. With Liam as a friend, I easily got along with many things, and I spent a lot of time with them. So I was often with them and all, but not always participating in ther discussions or activities. I liked being alone and observing all the other kids in my sixth-grade class or even more, regardless. Finally, I liked watching them interact with one another. I liked watching people act and interact with each other. Little by little, I began to notice more often a person my age who acted in a way that intrigued me, whether it was intentional on his part or not; he was calmer than all the others, even than I was. You had to notice him because he was more thoughtful than others, more measured in his actions, in everything he did. He acted like a mature child, and it suited him well. As a result, he was quite upright in his actions. He didn't do a lot of nonsense; he seemed very disciplined, very well put (put together). Quite right with himself, and precisely as I found out, I learned that he was the eldest son. He had many younger siblings, which made him someone who was extremely responsible. I understood why I was so interested because for me too, as the eldest child. I've always felt the need to behave in a certain way, to hold back, you know? Which was part of the norms in my family and how we were raised. So yes, I always had this little pressure, and the more I saw him, the more I observed him, the more he interested me. As I watched from afar, I would see more often and more frequently.

And one day, I made up my mind; I told myself yes, I was going to make him and me extremely close. I would force him as best I could. Even if at first, he wasn't interested. And even if at first, he didn't want to talk to me, I'd keep going toward him until he accepted me as a constant in his life as an important friend he couldn't forget or set aside or someone he should want to talk to. In fact, I wanted to be that person behind him all the time, and so I started to go toward him to get close to him. You're my buddy, I mean, you're one of my friends. I said it like that. And I got closer to him, I greeted him all the time. I don't know. I spoke as if we were old friends from primary school for quite a while, to get us closer. But I had decided, in fact, after all that stalking and psychopathic journey, to make him my friend, to always keep him close to me.

And that's how our friendship started, more by force than willingly on his side. Little by little, he got used to me being the person who decided to become his friend, who came close to him so much and all. He eventually accepted my friendship; my indirect friendship that was super strong and insistent, and we got closer bit by bit until he couldn't do without me and we were as close as we could be or rather as we once were. I realized that it was, just as I thought, the kind of person one could rely on who was upright in his behavior, always, and as time went on, I appreciated the existence, the bond, and the importance he had in my life even more. So there you go; I had never fully realized or attempted to realize why it mattered so much to me to be close to him, to be friends with him, to know him, to be in his company as closely as possible. I don't know. I never knew why I wanted him that much, but I wanted him with all my might; I made great efforts to make him a friend, and I never separated from him since.

<u>**Comment section**</u>

WdoBest_84_ : Wow, that was so sweet and so fucking boring. So you've had a crush forever.

Passeureby_102 : 🚶 Guetting boring again. 🚶

Seetrought93 : No. And no, I saw him as a good buddy.

WdoBest_84_ : Yeah, keep lying to yourself but don't take me for a fool.

Seetrought93 : You know what? Think whatever you want; you're wrong. My uncle (the youngest brother of my dadl died around that time, and I found he resembled him a bit in certain aspects, that's all. Nothing more. We where really close to. I often talked to him and we were joking often, really close.

WdoBest_84_ : Yeah, it's known; girls look for a husband who resembles daddy. Or someone as close as a daddy.

Seetrought93 : Fuck you.

WdoBest_84_ : Don't take it badly; I'm joking.

Seetrought93 : Hum.

WdoBest_84_ : I just think you and him would make a good couple; that's all.

Seetrought93 : That's not the issue.

WdoBest_84_ : Come on!

Seetrought93 : Okay, I was actually just going to get on that; just give me time to say everything as it comes to mind.

WdoBest_84_ : Alright, go ahead.

Seetrought93 : And it's good content for your novel; it's human.

WdoBest_84_ : You might be right.

Seetrought93 : I know since you don't have anything of a human you might need all the help you can get in that departement. I am here for that.

WdoBest_84_ : Fuck you.

Seetrought93 : I love you too.

WdoBest_84_ : That's MY line.

Seetrought93 : 😊

For the first time, we really had an irreparable argument, and I realize how important he had always been for me since the moment I decided he was someone important that I had to, with all my might, do everything to make him part of my circle. And how my mother, in fact, realized how important he was to me, so much so that I talked about him, so much that I told her who he was, how much I had talked about him at the beginning already. And how I insisted for her to meet him, that they should know each other and that she should realize too that he is one of the most cherished persons. And how I found him extraordinary. So that she would love him as much as I did and take him in as a son. This only served to strengthen my bond with him and my interest in our friendship and the strength with which I wanted him to be a part of my life. (And now I could have lost him for good, and I don't know if I can live with that because he has become a major constant in my life, and I don't think I'm ready to lose such an important constant in my life.) I've always wanted him to be an important and unalterable part of my life, no matter what happens. Whatever would happen. And this way, with my stupidity and my mess, I was about to lose one of the most important people in my life, and with this realization after that horrible argument, I truly realized how much I had messed up and that I needed to wake up and get him back, at least as a friend. Especially considering the way our argument ended.

Maybe in a way, Klaus had every reason to feel threatened by my relationship with Ray, especially in light of our discussion and its fallout. And, now that I have time to do nothing but reflect on myself and my feelings, I am sure he had every reason, even if he didn't really know how to behave, and I realized the importance of Ray and how we should be perceived by others, not just me. And that I had to find a way to regain at least his friendship, especially since that day, he had clearly confessed his feelings to me.

Flashback

I was extremely angry that Ray insulted and belittled me because of my choice to have a bit of fun with my own boyfriend. Our argument was violent, more violent than any we had ever had. More violent than I would have ever imagined we would have.

So you belittle me; I only represent so little in your eyes, and you assume you can talk down to me, scold me, and then decide to leave and make me the villain of the story. So I'm just a glorified whore, a stupid uninhibited brat who allows himself to be corrupted by his rich "boyfriend" making quotation marks with his fingers. I have no pride in your eyes; I just love sex. But in fact, I do what I want with my life, and it has nothing to do with you whatsoever.

- Why in front of my eyes?
- I live here too, and I never stopped you from bringing people home, and you've done it.
- But not like that, and even less so this often considering you also do it in his apartment.
- That's none of your business.
- Yes, but why do it in front of me?
- Because I can, and because I want to when it suits me.
- In what way?
- My room is right next door.
- So is mine. We live under the same roof. We've been best friends for over ten years. Of course, it concerns me, damn it. How can you allow yourself to say that I can't have my say?
- I care about you, so I can express myself if I feel like you are losing your way. I can't really stand by and watch you screw up your life right in front of my eyes; it's impossible. Especially... I really can't watch you get dragged and manipulated by that jerk who serves as your boyfriend. Who doesn't deserve you, which is turning you away from what you've always wanted for your life. I can no longer let you do this, especially if I know you don't feel compelled to listen to me and that my point of view has absolutely no value at all for you.
- And who is it that deserves me? All the girls I've hurt for no reason and especially— what else, finish your sentences, damn it.
- I'm sorry, but I'm going to leave and let you do this without any chance to help or stop you, especially knowing how much you mean to me. And how much I love and care about you. I'm sorry, but I can't anymore. I'm going to leave.

- I love you too, and I don't want you to go.
- You don't understand. You've always insisted that you have attraction only to girls, and so I told myself that you and I had no chance. Not because I did not know, I am your best friend you say things sometimes that gave it away but because I knew you just did not want to. Then I learned that not only are you bisexual like I taught and decided to own it, but that you still hid it from me preferring to spend your time with an idiot and screw up your life; I can't just stand there and watch you do it.
- What are you implying by saying that you thought we had no chance?
- I always held back, telling myself that between you and me, there could only be friendship, and I always held back as much as possible.
- Answer my fucking question.
- I'm leaving immediately.
- Answer my question.
- I already did. I love you.
- I love you too, but that's not the point.
- Yes, it is. I've been in love with you for a very long time.
- But I...you've always seen multiple....
- Anyway, there's nothing left to say. I'm leaving, and you can't say anything to stop me.
- But I... *He came in front of me he had a sad smile on his face.*
- I told you you were the only person I wanted to tell about those feelings back at the beach. Well I did not imagine it wouls go like this.

I opened my mouth to replie but nothing came out so I closed it back up.He moved to kiss me but finally decided to place a light kiss on my forehead. And then he walked out of the apartment without finishing his lunch, taking only his wallet and nothing more. It was later, when I wasn't there, that he came to get some things and messaged me.

Comment section

WdoBest_84_ : So you completely lied to me without batting an eye?

Seetrought93 : You don't see me batting my eyes.

WdoBest_84_ : You know what I meant by that. It's a saying.

Seetrought93 : Yes, but I wasn't ready to say it out loud.

WdoBest_84_ : Out loud?

Seetrought93 : By writing. Damn it, I'm so stupid.

WdoBest_84_ : Anyway, what do you think you'll do now?

Seetrought93 : I still don't know.With the mess you got into, you continue having doubts?

WdoBest_84_ : What a mess?

WdoBest_84_ : You clearly wrote that you felt super lonely during your Christmas holidays even while surrounded by your family.

Seetrought93 : And?

WdoBest_84_ : And, if for some reason, you end up forgetting and losing your feelings for Ray, do you think it will be better?

Seetrought93 : Do you think it's possible for me to forget him? I think i would love him all my life. No one else. And knowing it is even more scary.

WdoBest_84_ : Super difficult or rather impossible, I don't care it is beside the point. Do you think it will be better?

Seetrought93 : Well, yes.

WdoBest_84_ : No. The way I see it, you will never really not feel a certain degree of loneliness, even surrounded by your family, because you will have this huge secret. But above all, you will never really be yourself, and from what I understood, when you started to use this app, it was that you wanted to reclaim your true personality completely and become yourself again.

Seetrought93 : I know, but not at the expense of my relationship with my family.

WdoBest_84_ : I don't think it's fair that you have to choose between yourself and your family, and I think if your mother loves you and is exactly as you described her to me, she wouldn't want you to be as unhappy as you are right now. Even less so if it's because of her.

Seetrought93 : What do you think?

WdoBest_84_ : I think you don't give her enough credit.

Seetrought93 : I think she'll never be ready to accept it.

WdoBest_84_ : I think you've spent so much time being afraid that you can no longer see clearly. You are her son; she will never let you go. She can't lose you, and she doesn't want to, just like you. She will do everything to make it work. You owe it to her to trust her enough to tell her the truth.

Seetrought93 : You are making this sound so easy that I just want to trust you and jump into the unknown, but I don't know if I have enough courage to do it.

WdoBest_84_ : You know where all your courage will be?

Seetrought93 : Ray?

WdoBest_84_ : Yes, of course. If you have such a good reason to make it work, the courage will come with it.

Seetrought93 : I didn't let too much time pass, did I?

WdoBest_84_ : And for the tird time, He came to your place during the holidays knowing you would be there. I think you have every chance.

Seetrought93 : If you say so.

WdoBest_84_ : I say so.

Seetrought93 : Well, I'm going to keep mulling things over, and besides, I have another session tomorrow with Doctor Parker. I'll see if I feel better.

Passeureby_102 : 🚶 There is not wuch to think about you know ? You know already what you want just fight for it both of them dummy. 🚶

Drastic Choice: Ray or Mother. That's what I've been thinking about for a while now. For me, I had to choose between the two, and it seemed extremely impossible as a decision. How to choose between two so different but equally essential relationships? Then, after my session with Doctor Parker, she helped me realize one thing. I needed to stop talking about choices because there weren't really any. Not giving us a chance, me and Ray, wouldn't mean I'd suddenly stop being bisexual and lying to my mother. It would just give me one more excuse to keep lying to her and hiding, which would never be good for me, because the lie would remain. My choice had already been to lie to her about a part of my life, and my relationship with Ray, whatever it may be, wouldn't change anything. I had to deal with both. I had to be honest with both because otherwise, it would be as if I was choosing neither of the two and that I would lose both, and that's what I have been doing until now pushing them away, and I don't think it's wise to continue. I don't ever want to resent my own mother.

As much as I wanted to be with Ray, I also didn't want to disappoint my mother. That's why I found myself in this mess in the first place. And even if I was terrified about the future, I wasn't going to screw up. I didn't have all the answers, but I was going to do everything my heart dictated to me and see where that would lead me. I wanted to do my best for all those I loved.

When I arrived at the apartment, I couldn't help but run to his room to see if he was there and to see if I could redeem myself, but I noticed that he had taken more belongings and left me a note saying he was still at his uncle's and didn't plan to come home anytime soon, but he was looking for a new apartment as quickly as possible to leave me the apartment. I could only contact him in case of emergency. I felt my world collapse around me again. I felt suffocated, and I felt an intense panic at the thought of never being able to talk to him again. I felt a wave of immeasurable sadness, and I knew I had to get him back. I sat there on his bed, breathing slowly to calm down and come up with a plan. I refused to continue feeling this immense pain without reacting.

So, I walked out of his room and called him, and he answered, probably thinking it was an emergency:

- Don't hang up, listen to me until the end; I really need to talk to you. Just let me see you and tell you how I feel, what I need to say, and then you can decide.
- Okay.
- Can we meet to talk face to face?

- Um...
- Where do you want us to meet?
- Well.
- Luxembourg's Park today at 4 PM.
- Um, well...I...okay.
- Thank you very much.
- Um, yes, no worries.
- See you soon.

He didn't respond and hung up. I felt nervous. The meeting was in an hour, but I decided to head there immediately since it was twenty minutes away. And I was nervous; I was shaking everywhere and didn't yet know what to say to him. I didn't have the slightest plan. So I waited for him near the fountain as I had tested earlier, and I pondered what speech to hold as my anxiety grew. Then suddenly, I saw him in my line of sight. He walked hesitantly toward me, calm and classy as usual, upright and self-assured but with a rather tentative and hesitant gait. Seeing him made my stress disappear. I knew immediately what to do. I just ran toward him without any more thought and kissed him without ceremony. It was a long and sweet kiss where I attempted to pass all the love, affection, and tenderness I felt for him and where I lost myself in a shared moment of softness and tenderness until I lacked enough air to breath. When we broke apart, I was breathless and had a huge smile on my face:

- Wow, this kiss was long overdue. I felt like I was breathing completely again, although I was out of breath; who knows what that means? I felt like I was coming back to life. I think I lost my mind a bit.
- Yeah, it seems it was, wasn't it?
- I love you.
- Hum.
- I mean, I'm in love with you too. For as long as I can remember. *I felt like everything was crystal clear in my head again.*
- I think there are plenty of things to clarify before arriving at that point.
- You're right, I am going a bit fast.
- So?
- Are you okay if we sit? It seems I have a lot to tell you. I am not sure my own legs are still holding me well I am about to fall over.
- Okay, let's go.

After I poured everything out in one go as I did, we still needed to discuss the next events and especially how I was going to prepare for the conversation I was going to have with my mother. I just told him that I would take things one at a time, and I wasn't ready yet, so to give me a little time, and he agreed to that.

He had me sit on a good chair to really catch my breath. So I recounted everything I realized from the moment he left the apartment until this precise moment, what I really felt when I met him, all the thread of my thoughts, helped by Laura and my psychiatrist. I told him I wanted him back and that I was refusing his moving out and that he should come back today because I was losing my mind.

- A lot happened, didn't it?
- Yeah, you saw.
- She's right, I came to see your mother because I wanted to see you, so I think I was super angry too when you left.
- I held a bit of resentment for you, but at the same time, I was relieved because I didn't know how long I could keep it together if you had stayed.
- Me neither.
- So if I understood correctly, you plan to talk to your mother and come out.
- Exactly. But not just yet. I still have several sessions with the psychiatrist to complete before I can do that.
- I understand.
- 'I've missed you so much that you can't even imagine.
- Come here. *He opened his arms, and I snuggled against his chest.*
- Perfect.
- I know. When I indirectly confessed my feelings to you at the beach last summer, I never thought that day would come.
- I suppose neither did I.
- I love you too.
- You're coming back with me.
- Clearly, I don't think I could sleep anywhere else but in our apartment on a day like today.
- Isn't that so?
- Let's stay here a little longer anyway.
- With pleasure.

I'm not really sure how exactly it happened, but we stayed on the bench, hand in hand, for a good ten minutes, and then by mutual agreement, without even giving each other a sign, we got up together to take the transports to return to the apartment. On the transport or even while walking, we didn't exchange a single word. Not even when I had to look for the keys to the apartment in question.

During the ride, I couldn't stop reflecting on what I had decided to take (Bad habits die hard). Did I make the right decision? And even more importantly, what did I decide? Sure, I had confessed my feelings to him, but that's all. Okay, we kissed and held hands for 45 minutes, but that's all. I didn't know if technically we were dating now or if we needed to discuss it. I didn't know where to go in my head.

In short, the fact is that we returned together, hand in hand, to the apartment, and we were stuck in the living room like two idiots for 2 or 3 minutes. I clearly didn't know if I should withdraw my hand or say something. I just knew I loved feeling the connectivity between our intertwined hands and the warmth radiating from his body to mine. Just as I was thinking about withdrawing my hand with a heavy heart, he pulled it back toward him and kissed me fully, not that I was complaining.

- I wanted to do that the whole ride.
- Oh really?
- Clearly not you.
- I don't know.
- Really. So do you want more?
- No, not at all, I don't...

Before I even had time to react or finish my sentence, he pressed his lips against mine again. Again, without me having anything to complain about it. We must have stayed there in the middle of the living room for a good while kissing. Then suddenly, he stopped and pulled his hand away. The cold grip of his hand left me, and so I stayed there just standing. I felt like a complete idiot at that moment. When he noticed I wasn't moving while he had already changed his clothes, he moved closer to me.

- What are you still doing here? Go get changed so we can cook something together.
- Um, yes, of course.
- By the way, what do you want to eat tonight?
- I don't know; it's up to you.

- Just like I want today. And what if we drop the dinners and just go straight to bed?
- You're really an idiot. Chop the onions while I handle the carrots and tomatoes.
- With pleasure, Willy.
- Hum.
- You know ? *He said while chopping the onions like I asked.*
- Hum.
- I was loosing my mind waiting, hoping you'd call me, what took you so long ?
- I am an idiot.
- That you are. But you are my idiot.
- No you didn't. Anyway, Laura thinks you came home on chrismas to see me not to talk to mom.
- It't the friend you made on that app you just told me about ?
- Yes!
- She is right. I needed to see you.
- Since when do you talk so sweetly ?
- You don't know my romantic part.
- Stop it I am blushing. I am not use to this.
- Get used to it I am not holding back anymore.

He seemed serous while saying it. He even stop to look me in the eyes while talking before placing a light kiss on my forehead and going back to his onions. I was dumbfounded.

We ended up watching some episodes of South Park while eating. When I returned to the couch after clearing the table, he was already well settled with his arms wide open so I could snuggle up comfortably against his chest. Which I immediately did. I couldn't be more comfortable than that. In short, we had a super good evening, and around midnight, I didn't really want to go to bed even knowing I had class. But it had to be because the class in question was very important for my average and interesting.

So, around midnight, I moved away from his chest to stretch and stand up to go to bed.

- It's time for me to go to sleep; I have class at 8:30 AM, and since I want to keep my struggling grades up, I'd better sleep enough, I said yawning.
- Oh yeah, that's right; you told me. Well, let's go to sleep. Your room or mine.
- Um...
- My bed is bigger, I'd say, so my room?

- What do you mean, your room? What are you talking about?
- Well, I'm asking where you want us to sleep tonight.
- Like together?
- Well, yes. Why? Do you prefer to sleep alone?
- Um, well, I don't know.
- It's up to you, but I would have thought you'd miss me as much as I had missed you and you'd like to sleep together, but well, if you don't want to, I'll withdraw the invitation.
- No, not at all. I'll say your room.
- Great then. I'm going to brush my teeth.
- Okay, I'm going to get changed and go straight to bed.
- Wait for me before you sleep.
- I'll try.

I went to change in my room. I didn't know what to wear because normally I sleep naked, but I thought that wasn't really a good idea at the moment, so I finally opted for a large t-shirt with my boxers. Very simple, no too much clothing. Then I went to lie down under the covers in his room against the wall. I was waiting for him, but when I heard him approaching, I closed my eyes like an idiot and stayed there without moving. He undressed, keeping only his boxers, and slid next to me after turning off the lights. He first came above me and whispered :

- Good night. I know you're not sleeping yet. I'm super happy that you're finally sleeping here.
- I love you. See you tomorrow.

Then I nestled my head against his chest. It was in this position that I finally fell asleep.

The next morning, when I opened my eyes, I wasn't exactly in the same position, but I was facing the same direction, and when I lifted my eyes a bit, he was there looking at me sleeping, and smiling.

- Hello.
- What a creep.
- Seriously.
- Well, you were watching me sleep, so yes.

- On the other hand, I can't get up if you're holding me so tightly.
- Yes, I suppose that's what makes you watch me sleep like a creep.
- Exactly.
- Well, that's nice and all, but I need to go to my class. I'm going to take a shower.
- Okay, but first, good morning kiss?
- No way. You have morning breath. I don't kiss anyone in the morning. I don't do this kind of white guy shit.
- Oh, seriously, jerk.
- Like you say; I'm really funny.
- Hum.

And just by saying it, I got up to go brush my teeth and take a shower. In the meantime, Ray pretended to sulk, following me everywhere like a kid. At some point he disappeared in his room before coming back but I was too busy to pay attention at the moment. When I finished getting ready, I gave him a little kiss and grabbed my bag. I was about to leave after putting on my coat when he said:

- You're leaving like that without saying anything else? And especially without even apologizing.
- Excuse me, baby. So sorry, I have to go. But I'll be coming back soon.
- I don't care.
- I love you too. *All said in a childish voice to annoy him. And I can say it worked.*
- I turned to him and realized he was dressed.
- Wait, why are you dressed ?
- I am coming with you.
- But you don't have class until eleven.
- I know ! But I want to walk you there. You don't mind me doing that, do you ?
- I would like that very much.

I left the house with a big smile on my face and his hand in mine.We went down the elevator and out of the building holding hands and it might sound a little childish and or ridiculous but I have never felt better.

That validation I got addicted to and that pushed me in Klaus's hands, well it was nothing compared to the feeling I got from just that simple gesture with him. With Ray. It ment mote and felt better and it was for the world to see and it was incredible. I could not stop myself from smiling ear to ear.

Ray realised I was in some sort of transe and got me out of it by asking :

- Is everything ok you are smiling like a lunatic.
- I am fine. No better, I feel amazing.
- Ok ?
- Just being outside holding hand with you is enough for me to be incredibly happy.
- And I am the creepy one.
- Come on I am trying to be cute here.
- I can see that. But if you don't stop smiling like that I might not let you go to Uni and take you back home.
- Take a chill pill.
- I told you I have been chilling for far to long I am done chilling. I am going to do whatever I want now.
- I can't wait to see that.
- You might regret saying that.
- I don't think so.
- Ok ! *I smiled at him and he added.* I tought you might get tired of me being so needy like you usually are.
- With you I don't think it will be possible.
- Happy to hear that. but you will tell me if it happens, right ? I saw it happen a lot so I confess I am A little worried by that side of you.
- I never felt that with you. Sometimes even Liam and Antoine annoy me a little and I feel like I might be tired of seeing them. But it never happened with you never. I usually want to spend even more time with you. I can't believe I did not figure it out until now.
- It is not a big deal as you know now.
- But I lost so much time.
- Yeah well, nothing can be done about it now.
- Hum I suppose you are right.
- I know I am. *He stop and placed a warm kiss on my forehead before continuing working. And then my lunatic like smile came back.*

We walked in silence enjoying being in each other's presence. Exchanging once in a comment or another perfectly content with our little scroll.

<u>Comment section :</u>

WdoBest_84_ : How cute and boring.

Seetrought93 : Fuck off !

WdoBest_84_ : Just saying no need to be rude.

When we arrived and pasted the gate of the university I turned to Ray.

- So you go to the left and I to the right. See you tonight ?
- No I can go with you until we attend the front of your classroom. I don't start before another hour or two I don't have to leave already.
- You are right... Let's go then!

We continued walking hand and hand until arriving in front of the building. When we were about to go in I heard a voice calling my name. I recognized it immediately.

- Klaus ? *I turned To find his gray eyes looking at me intensely and then turned darker when he realized it was Ray standing next to me and worse that we were holding hands.*
- So I was right. He wanted you from the start. *He said staring at our joined hands.*
- Yes, long before you even came into the picture. *Answered Ray.*
- Ray please, *I said trying to calm the situation.* Klaus what are you doing here?
- Well you've been ignoring me for three weeks now I actually need to talk to you. I can't loose you Will. I love you.
- He does not feel the same way. *Answered Ray trying to place himself in front of me to shield me. I unlinked our hands and move in front of a fuming Klaus.*
- He does not love you, he came to me first. Did not even consider you at first. All his first real experiences were with me so you can shut your stupid mouth. *He said almost yelling.*
- What did you just say ? *Ray was moving again to face him. But I stopped him one more time before concentrating on Klaus.*
- Klaus, you and I are done. I don't want to see you again. Stop looking for me. I am with Ray now.
- No I can't accept that, you belong with me. You do remember how well we fit together.
- We don't.

- You can't say that. You can't be happy with that boring idiot.
- I don't agree with you talking about him like that. He is better than you can ever be an even more for me.
- You mean to tell me I was right from the start for being weary of him.
- I suppose I owe you some apologies for that. Yes you were. I love him like I never have loved anyone else and probably would never.
- I see that I can't do anything to change your mind or make you realize what a stupid mistake you are making.
- It is not a mistake.
- Well let's agree to disagree on that.
- Goodbye Klaus.
- I am leaving since you seem to be done with me.
- I am. *He then turned and leaved without another word. I turned to find Ray with a big smile looking at me with pride.*
- What ?
- What you just said you meant it ?
- I meant everything but can you be specific ?
- The thing about loving me more than you did anybody and never would. That part.
- Of course I meant it. Do you still not realize that ?
- Well it feels amazing to hear.
- You are welcome. *He took my hand back in his and then went inside the building together.*

Comment section :

WdoBest_84_ : Wait, wait. Are you going to tell me all about your week?

Seetrought93 : Yes, of course.

WdoBest_84_ : And is it similar to everything you just told me?

Seetrought93 : Yes.

WdoBest_84_ : I don't want to know then.

Seetrought93 : What? How come?

WdoBest_84_ : Your sappy stories give me hives. Please shut up.

Seetrought93 : What?

WdoBest_84_ : Like, you just better stop writing.

Seetrought93 : But that is good book material.

WdoBest_84_ : No way.

WdoBest_84_ : When you disappeared for a week, I thought you got dumped. But you were just too busy getting high.

Seetrought93 : No.

WdoBest_84_ : By the way, tell me how it happened?

Seetrought93 : What?

WdoBest_84_ : Sex stuff. That is good book material.

Seetrought93 : No thanks.

WdoBest_84_ : But yes.

Seetrought93 : No.

WdoBest_84_ : Besides, doesn't he know you usually sleep naked?

Seetrought93 : Yes, he pointed that out, and I told him I wasn't sure why I thought it was weird.

WdoBest_84_ : And?

Seetrought93 : Well, he said it wouldn't bother him and especially it would save him some work every time he wanted to jump on me in bed.

WdoBest_84_ : Good thinking, I like him.

Seetrought93 : Pervert.

WdoBest_84_ : Thanks for the compliment.

Seetrought93 : You're really annoying.

WdoBest_84_ : Anyway, where is Prince Charming right now so you'll deign to talk to me again?

Seetrought93 : He's in class this afternoon. So I'm alone.

WdoBest_84_ : I figured.

Seetrought93 : Well, I'm going to keep remembering my week.

WdoBest_84_ : And I'm going to disconnect. Bye.

Seetrought93 : I can also tell you a bit of sex stuff, I'm sure you'd really be interested for your novel.

WdoBest_84_ : Fine, listening for now.

Seetrought93 : Pervert.

On Friday, we decided to stay home and eat as much junk food as possible while watching loud horror movies. In short, best date ever. So we stayed on the couch from 6:30 pm to 2 am without even realizing it, all wrapped up in each other's arms on the couch under the blanket.

<u>**Comment section :**</u>

WdoBest_84_ : Becoming boring again.

Seetrought93 : Fuck off.

WdoBest_84_ : Okay, living.

Seetrought93 : 😖

WdoBest_84_ : Fine. Continue.

Seetrought93 : Good.

So around two o'clock, I started yawning, and he noticed. How sweet is he?

<u>Comment section</u>

WdoBest_84_ : Really? Again?

Seetrought93 : Sorry, too tempting.

WdoBest_84_ : Ass.

Seetrought93 : Love you too. Anyway,

He asked me if I wanted to go to bed. I said yes, and we both went to brush our teeth. I took the opportunity to take a shower. And when I finished, he was in the bedroom under the blanket. I was putting on a top to go to bed again when he said:

- Another t-shirt?
- Yes, why?
- Don't you usually sleep naked?
- Yes, but I thought it was a bit weird and too soon. Don't you think?
- Not really, and besides you don't sleep well when you're dressed, so forget it and get naked.
- Okay, but don't start drooling.
- Way too much ego, I'd say.
- Okay, we'll see how long you can last all soft.

So I started undressing very slowly while dancing slightly just to annoy him, but from the look on his face, I could tell I had a big effect on him, and I felt his breathing become shorter and more erratic.

- Are you sure you don't want me to get dressed again?
- No, just come join me right now.
- I really don't want to.
- Stop being such a tease.
- Okay, I will be kinder to you.

I said as I moved closer to the bed to lie down. But before I even touched the bed in question, he had already violently pulled me towards the bed.

- I like where this is going.
- Shush or I'll stop.
- Fine, dick.

I didn't even have time to protest when he was already kissing me. It seemed like he had been waiting for this for a while and couldn't hold back anymore. I don't need to describe what happened next. Just let me say that I needed a second shower, if you know what I mean.

<u>Comment section :</u>

WdoBest_84_ : Not really what I expected, you little jerk. You're really the worst.

Seetrought93 : I know. I love annoying you.

WdoBest_84_ : Are you mocking me?

Seetrought93 : Exactly.

WdoBest_84_ : Fine, I'm leaving now. Ciao.

Seetrought93 : Bye.

I woke up on Saturday morning with Ray starring at me with red eyes. I couldn't understand what was wrong with him. I try to move to stand up and ask him just that but he stopped me and seemed even more tense.

- Don't you move. He said in a horse voice.
- What is wrong with you ? *I said a little startled.*
- A part from the fact that you have been rubbing on my Dick for the last ten to five minutes nothing.
- Oh ! *I said not really knowing how to react.* I am sorry.
- Hum.

- Should I stand up or ?
- Well, you can at least give me the time to settle down if not offering to take care of it.
- Take care of it ? *I said in a little voice.*
- Don't act prude. *Without thinking too much of it I lowered my hand until I could feel his hot member through his boxer briefs. At that precise moment I felt his breath stop for a few seconds before coming back he looked at me with interrogation in his eyes.*
- What do you think you are do ... He could not finish because I had started moving up and down his length.
- Taking my responsibilities. Was it not what you wanted ?
- Well !

He could not make complete sentences because of my movements and I was enjoying the expressions passing through his face. To make matter worse I put my hand under his boxer He started really blushing furiously from the ears and spitting muffled insulte. I was really enjoying myself but soon enought he got tired of being the only victim. When he got use to my bullying he was able to stop me and overturn me to be the one on top of me.

- You are such and bully.
- I stand up very well to those.

And after saying that he started kissing me furiously, on the lips, the neck, the chest, the stomach, everywhere he could put his lips on. I was the one losing my mind now. I have become a real mess of sounds and I was not being really discreet. It seemed there was a logic to his madness because his frantic kissing was neutralisant me efficiently but also leading to something. I was to occupied enjoying his assauts to know when he undressed me but I found out when I felt his mouth around my érections. For A moment there I forgot to breath a had a violent muscle réaction that made move my waist in such a way, that my Dick went deeper into his traught. He did not even Flinch. he just settled my hips and started moving slowly up and down my lenght. I was loosing my mind before but not I couldn't even tell were I was anymore. He was completely undoing me. I could not even make sense of how intensely good I was feelling.

- P... P... Pleeease s... s...top. Huhhhh... I... I want ... I... I want to take... Huhhh care of y...y...you too. *I said stuttering, making the utmost effort to manage that simple sentence.*

He moved along my length two time more before shoping to look up at me with a smile.

- What did you think of my standing up to you ?
- J...Jerk ! *I said trying take back control of my breathing.* You... Huhhh... You are too good at that.
- Hum also I had dreamt of doing that for a long time.
- Hum.
- So what was that about returning the favor.
- I would love too. *He smiled and stood up on the bed to get naked.*

When he released his erection from it's confinements I could not hold up a gasp. He was big and long, I could tell went touching him earlier but not to this extend. like really big. When he placed himself, kneeling, in front of my face, I attemped to take hold of him with one hand could not close it on it. I was clearly impressed. I opended wide and took him in my mouth and started moving slowly trying to take his whole lenght un my throat. His grunting were encouraging me to go for it. At first he left me take control and go at my own pace. But, soon enough he put his right hand on my head digging into my curly hair and mooving my head first slowly but then quicker and quicker until I could not breath and making a mess of my face. And then he stop out of nowhere and got completly out of my mouth, giving me a little time to take back my breathing before trusting deep inside again. It took me by surprise and provoked a gag reflexe but I held on while he starded mooving again. He did that once or twice more. Before stopping he said out of breath :

- I need to be inside you now. *His voice was horse. I could tell he was having a hard time controlling himself at that moment.*

We laid there catching our breath for a minute before moving down to place himself on top of me to kiss me exploring every inch of my mouth with his tongue. And yet again Without any kind of warning he stop letting me gasping, panting and longing again while he was searching through his night stand for what I finally realized to be lubrifiant. Then after wetting his fingers and pushed first his index finger inside me slowly moving in and out rapide increasing pace and then introduced a second and ten third finger. It was getting more and more difficult for me to breath properly through all the sounds and gasp leaving my mouth without my permission. He then stop abruptly and replaced gis fingers with his erection without missing a bit. I felt immediately the difference in thickness and length but I was not able to express it with my moaning before yet again exploring my mouth with his tongue.

I was assaulted with pletore of sensations all at once and it was difficult to concentrate on any one of them. I was completely lost in the pleasure. And his pace seemed to keep increasing. He was relently pounding inside me and I was totally appréciation of his attention seeing how loud I was when he stoped kissing. At some point he lowered his head and started kissing my nipples. I became even louder and pried to push his head but he was yed again relentlessly even bitting them a little. T did not take me a long time to finally come while streaming on top of my lungs and he joined me soon enough grunting almost as loudly as me directly in my ear after trusting another two times.

We stayed there, him on top and inside me and laying on the soaking bedsheet for a good time trying to catch our breaths. He was the first one to talk.

- A bath before round two ?
- Round two in the bath ? *I answer.*
- I like how you think. But more seriously we should wash out and change the sheets.
- Yes but I want to stay like this a little longer.
- Agreed. *He standed on his left hand and looked me in the eyes before putting a light kiss on my forehead and then on my lips.* I love you, you know that?

I was stunned and said nothing for a moment before answering back that I loved him too. He smiled and settled back down and attempted to hold me even closer. We stayed like that for at least another thirty minutes before leaving to take a bath and as anticipated it was not a simple one.

<u>Comment section :</u>

WdoBest_84_ : How steamy I love it and the details ? Miam !

Seetrought93 : Pervert.

WdoBest_84_ : No, I just like it hot and steamy like normal people.

Seetrought93 : Yeah right, pervert.

WdoBest_84_ : If you say so.

Seetrought93 : Now you can't say I don't give you material for your books.

WdoBest_84_ : Yeah, yeah. So can I just make a copyright and paste ?

Seetrought93 : Of course not !

WdoBest_84_ : Bummer.

Seetrought93 : Whatever.

Passeureby_102 : 🏃 Too much info here 🏃

_ A week later _

I have been swimming in deadlines and sleeping extremely late for weeks now, always stuck in my old room working.

I was still swamped this wednesday when Ray popped his head to check up on me.

- Still going at it.
- Yep.
- And is it helping out ?
- With mom's disappearing act from my life yep a little. But I miss hanging out with you. *I said turning to face him, leaving my plans for a moment. I gave him a sad smile and he entered the room to come stand in front of me.*
- I am just here. I am going to lay on that bed just behind you, watching you work just after taking a shower. *He said all that with his hand in my hair. He loves playing with them. And I love it when he does.*
- Yeah but I would have loved to take the shower with you.
- I would have love that too but I prefer for you to finish quickly to be able to sleep earlier than later.
- Hum. *He bent and placed a kiss on my forehead, staying there for a little while before leaving.*
- I am back in a few minutes.
- Ok.

He left and came back about thirty minutes later in a simple t-shirt and shorts, with a book in his hands. He gave a kiss before going to lay on the bed behind me to read comfortably. I loved having him there and he knew it so he always did. Even before we started dating he would come and keep me company when I had a lot to work on and distract me once in a while with small talk. He is just the best. Anyway it was the same, this time he interrupted me by telling me about what he was reading and I would give a little comment before going back to work.

About three hours later I was pretty much done for the night. I realized I haven't heard Ray talk for a while and turned to look at him. Sure enough he fell asleep on his back with a hand on his head, with the book on his stomach. So adorable. I approached him and squatted in front of him to watch him sleep.

He looked so peaceful in his sleep, with his beautiful hair crowning his face, his long lashes making a little shadow under his eyes, his mouth frozen in a light smile. I could stay there looking at him for hours on end. I just got his creepy tendencies now. We are now a couple of creeps.

Suddenly he started moving and slowly opened his eyes to show his beautiful gray-green eyes. Upon seeing me he smiled and then a small chuckle came from his mouth.

- So I am not the only creep anymore.
- No I was just thinking that we were definitely a couple of creeps
- Hum.
- Wanna go to bed.
- With pleasure.

He stood up, I did the same and we headed to the room completely undressed leaving only my boxers, and laid on his chest after giving him a kiss and went to sleep. It did not take us a long time to fall asleep.

Comment section :

WdoBest_84_ : You really don't deserve that guy do you ?

Seetrought93 : I don't.

Passeureby_102 : 🧍 You really do not. 🧍

WdoBest_84_ : And to think you made him wait so long.

Seetrought93 : Stop it. I know I was wrong but I was dealing with a lot.

WdoBest_84_ : Yeah right. You are just a little too cowerdly.

Seetrought93 : I am.

WdoBest_84_ : Good to see you know. Take good care of him, he is a catch.

Seetrought93 : He definitely is and I definitely will.

WdoBest_84_ : Good.

_ Two weeks later _

Entry Friday

Guess what just happened? I was peacefully sitting on the couch reading while Ray was cooking when the doorbell rang. I went to open it, and behind the door was my mother, who had come for an impromptu visit just because she can, all smiling. Reality checked too soon. I really didn't know how to react.

- Surprise!!!
- Oh, now that's a surprise. What are you doing here, Mom?
- I see you're thrilled to see me.
- Of course, come in. Would you like something to drink ,
- Yes, some water, please.
- Ray is in the kicthen.
- Alright, thank you.

I went to pour her some water in the kitchen while she took the opportunity to warmly greet the prodigal child, just as usual.

- Good evening, my dear, how are you?
- I'm fine, thank you, and you?
- Great. I'm happy to see that at least one of you is glad to see me.
- But Mom, I'm happy you're here; I was just shocked.

- Of course.
- Do you want to eat something special? We can order something.
- No, I'd rather have my son cook for me. That okay with you, Ray?
- Of course.
- I knew I could always count on my son.
- I'm still here, you know?
- Don't be jealous; it doesn't suit you.
- Thank you very much, Mom.

The rest of the evening passed like that, with me as the third wheel to the lovely mother-son reunion of Ray and my mother.

<u>Comment section :</u>

WdoBest_84_ : Jealousy is not a pretty color on you.

Seetrought93 : Fuck you, you really are the worst sometimes.

WdoBest_84_ : I know, I'm super funny.

Seetrought93 : Hum.

WdoBest_84_ : Anyway, more seriously, how's home now that she's here?

Seetrought93 : Well, Ray and I are sleeping separately, and we have to act like friends at home.

WdoBest_84_ : Super cool. Hum.

Seetrought93 : Yep. Sometimes it's really hard not to jump on him.

WdoBest_84_ : Ew. I don't care.

Seetrought93 : Ok make up your mind you like it is steamy or not.

WdoBest_84_ : Shut it already.

Passeureby_102 : Now that he finally did what he was suppose to for years he is becoming even more boring than before.

The-hot-girl_42 : Yeah and so full of himself flaunting his perfect boyfriend.

Jerom_666_ : Our hot girl is actually feeling jealous.

Joker-99- : It did not get better hera with time did it ?

Jerom_666_ : Not really.

_ Three weeks later _

When my mother came, we knew we felt slightly worried, of course, but we said we would try to hold back from being too demonstrative, not to give her too much ideas while she was here and because I wasn't ready yet and also it wasn't the time or the way to tell her. So, at first, it seemed possible to hold back, to act like teenagers. But the only problem was our respective consciences, especially mine, because I struggled; it was killing me not being able to talk to my mother about something so important happening in my life.

Then one day, what had to happen happened. One evening when she went out for a walk, Ray and I took the opportunity to have a bit of alone time together. We didn't even hear her come back into the house. The fact is that she saw us kissing, and everything suddenly went down the shitter. I didn't know how to react since everything was going wrong.

That was the first time I saw her so angry, so upset, so virulent. She was completely out of control. Our arguments were really violent, and she told me to take my things and follow her to a hotel to spend the evening. Then she would make sure I would stay with my aunt who lived extremely far from me, like 1 hour and 30 minutes from my university and about 1 hour and 30 minutes from here too. At that moment, Ray came out of his room. It was clear he had been listening to us talk. He offered to go to his uncle's house, who lived much closer, half the distance, 45 minutes. That it wouldn't bother him to leave. She accepted. Coldly, she told him, "Fine, leave in 15 minutes; I don't want to see you anymore." I had never seen her talk to Ray like that, the beloved child, the adored one, whom she treated much better than her own son. All of this pained me deeply, and moreover, I absolutely disagreed with Ray being forced to leave. I responded violently that she had no right to kick him out of his own apartment, that she had absolutely nothing to say. It was Ray who calmed me down, telling me he preferred to leave.

In the end, he thought it was time for him to go, and at that moment, seeing my mother's anger, I thought it might be better, and I kept quiet. Even though I didn't completely agree with myself. Once a pleaser, always a pleaser, right? So I just stayed silent. From the first violent reaction of my mother, as soon as Ray told me he was okay with leaving. That night, we went to bed, and I didn't sleep. I don't think my mother slept either.

Neither did Ray, he told me later on. but I couldn't contact him because my mother had taken my phone like I was still a teenager. Because she said I had to use it, not talk to Ray for a while and get this nonsense out of my head. So there I was, without a phone like a kid. There was nothing I could do, nothing I could say, nothing I could do about it. You have to be sure that if an African mother says to you, "Give me your phone", you give me your phone, you shut up and go with your tail between your legs to your room without speaking, no matter how old you are.

As a result, I couldn't sleep, I couldn't talk to Ray. I was completely depressed. The weekend was horrible. My mother and I didn't talk to each other, she cooked and left everything in the kitchen, we never ate at the same time (like a tacit agreement).

We took turns, pretty much saying nothing. We had organized ourselves for the rest of that week. The only rule was to avoid talking at all costs.

I really couldn't talk much, I couldn't do much, I was just depressed, I was lost, I didn't know what to do and my appointment with the parker doctor was on Friday, so I went. Totally lost. I told her what had happened and what a violent discussion it had been, how I still felt bad inside, like I was a lost teenager again, how I felt that the depression I'd managed to overcome not too badly about three months earlier, was coming back, that I really didn't know how to react, that I was lost.

And Dr. Parker advised me to talk to my mother again and tell her exactly how bad I felt, how unhappy I was.

And that's what I decided to do on Saturday after 12 p.m., just after lunch. Strangely enough, that Saturday, we'd had lunch at the same time, on the same table, just the same silence.

I could hear forks scraping, dishes moving in dishes, dishes, in short, the normal sounds of people eating. Hm. In this oppressive silence, I had. I could feel my resolve waning. But I took my courage in both hands. I put my fork and knife down beside my plate, turned to my mother and looked her straight in the eye. Then I said to her.

– Mom, I've got something important to tell you. "So I took all my time telling her everything that had happened since the meeting with Klaus without going into details."

Not exactly what happened that day, but I told her that well, he kissed me. In front of the others. In the box, I felt something that I'd started dating him and my fight with Ray. The very fact that this summer, where I'd returned, was why I'd had so much. I was also vague in my answers because we'd had a fight. I'd tell him about my discomfort and the pain I was feeling, and how it hurt me not to talk to him. I told her everything, in fact, everything that had happened up to that day. So she just stood there in silence, listening to me, and she didn't say a word and let me talk until I'd finished, and then she just stood there without moving, even after I'd finished talking.

And I'd been talking for what seemed like an eternity. And when she opened her mouth again, she told me and she said she understood what I'd been through, that it was something horrible, that I'd had an experience that I'd found exciting and then I'd found it. I thought it was a norm, that I'd mistaken my friendship with Ray for something it wasn't, and begged me to change my mind, not to go down that path, to go back to being his normal son. And then, and this is where I lost it, I couldn't understand how she could say something like that to me after hearing what I had to tell her. How had she come to that conclusion?

– I'm sorry, Mom, but I haven't been completely honest with you in a long time. Now, I am for the first time, and you're telling me to start lying again, to go back to a life where I didn't recognize myself and where I'm still going. Losing myself and lying to myself, you want me to stay there, suffering and unhappy for the rest of my life. How can you ask me something so horrible, so impossible, so mean you think you're my mother for real, you think you behave like a mother? You really think you're behaving like a good mother? I don't understand how you can say something like that to me.

She was completely overwhelmed by what I'd just said.

I actually realised I did some real damage to myself during that period, when I saw the tears streaming down my face, by understanding how serious I was, by talking about depression and pain.

She finally shut up completely and waited a few more minutes before coughing. Well, to what extent? I'd been lying to her all these years. My whole life, her.

She doesn't say another word. She goes into the guest room where she was sleeping and a few minutes later comes back with my phone, which she hands back to me without saying a word. Then when it was time to go she said she was living alone and did not need me to come with her to the train station. Then she went back to her room to take care of her things and finally put them away because she was leaving that evening.

That evening, when she finished packing and it was time for her to leave. She came up to me and said,

- Have a nice rest of the year! *She gave me a peck on the cheek and was about to leave.*
- Do you realize that I'm going to call Ray and he'll be back? You do realize that, don't you?

She didn't answer, but she didn't take my phone either. She didn't react, in fact. She didn't say a word, just paused for a few minutes.

Then she moved on and left the apartment, closing the door behind her. I insist on saying Yes, Ray's coming back. And I know. Because I absolutely can't live without him.

But the door remained closed. I knew she was behind what we were hearing. I'd heard it was that she hadn't moved, that she'd just stood there. She didn't say anything, and it was at that very moment that she left completely for the train station to go back to Bordeaux.

On tuesday, I was pacing in the living room when Ray got in from work. It's been two days since my mom got back home and I had no news. What was worse, nothing seemed to have changed with the other members of my family. She told nothing to my dad or siblings. I did not know if it was better or worse. Seeing me in that state Ray rushed to put his bag down and give me a hug from behind.

- She did not write to you all day, yesterday, or this morning ?
- No she did not. *I said putting my arms on his hands to hug him back.*
- And it is sort of your ritual to write to each other every monday to wish each other a good week.
- Yep our own ritual that she forgot about.

- Did you send her something ?
- I did.
- No response ?
- No.
- I am sorry love... I am sure she is in the same state as you, and confused too.
- Maybe but it still hurts to know that she is ignoring me.
- I get that love, I do but you have to give her some time.
- I don't want to have to.
- It is what it is. You can't do anything about it now. I can go back home now.
- No you can't. You told me you had a lot to do lately.
- Yes but ...
- She also needs time.
- I know. *He turned me, kissed me on the lips and hugged me again.* I know it is hard but you two are going to make it. You don't give enough credit to your mother.
- You think so ?
- I know so. Now let's cook dinner.
- Ok.

He kissed me again and he went into our room to change and we did just that. He spent the rest of the evening trying to reassure me, and it kind of worked at some moments but there was always a tough coming back to me from time to time. What if she never comes around ?

<u>Comment section :</u>

WdoBest_84_ : She will, do not worry, she seems to love you too much to be able to push you away for too long.

Seetrought93 : Thank you for saying that.

WdoBest_84_ : Pleasure. I am still here if you need.

Seetrought93 : You are being too kind. It is frightening.

WdoBest_84_ : Shut it.

Seetrought93 : Ok mam.

The next day, I decided to call my siblings to take the temperature of the house a little. The one to respond was Aiden, his sister of course never takes the phone, always listening to loud music in her room. Tiring, anyway he responded quickly enough with excitement as always.

- Hello bros what a nice surprise calling about mom ?
- Huh, mom ? How did you figure it out ?
- Since coming back on Sunday she's been brooding and could not bother to respond when we ask about you or Ray for that matter. She sure had an argument with her golden boy. So you, calling three days later out of the blue clearly something is wrong. You don't call, you text.
- Fair enough. How is she ?
- Well, like I said she is brooding and not really smiling lately either. She seems to always be in her head thinking about something.
- I see she is still considering I suppose it is good news.
- Good news about what ? You have yet to tell me exactly what happened.
- I am not sure I want to talk about it on the phone.
- Not fair it will be years before you come back.
- You are exaggerating.
- Figure of speech.
- Whatever.
- So tell me. Or better yet tell us I am going to Ariane's room to shut the stupid kpop music down. Done. What did I say?.
- I don't know.
- You want me to say what I think ?
- I am listening. It has to be extremely hugefor her to be mad at both you and Ray since he became a sore spot for her too.
- So ?
- You guys finally decided to date.
- Huhh ?
- It is not my idea. Ariane says you guys look at each other in a weird romantic way all the time so I thought that might be it.
- Yeah you guys were too much obvious. Hey Will, how are you ? And, you Aiden rude, you can't just cut taemin's song like that.
- Ok fine whatever. So, Will are we right ?
- Well yeah you are. I can't believe it is obvious to everyone and not me.

- You and mom I would say.
- Yeah !
- Where is Ray by the way. I want to see my hot brother in law.
- In the shower.
- Then what are you doing here talking to us. Go join him you lost enough time don't you think ?
- Ariane !
- What she is right. From what she told me it has been going on for a while now.
- Don't always follow her in her stupidity.
- We are twins. Anyway, you have to come back soon to tell us everything about it.
- Whatever.
- Now go.
- No wait. Can you not tell anything to dad for now please. One disapproving parent is enough for now.
- Fine but what if he asks if we talked to you ?
- Yeah he did that yesterday. We said we heard nothing but now we did.
- Yeah just tell him to call me then. I'm not up for now but we will see.
- Can I have a cute photo of you guys pleeeease ?
- No.
- Come on Will, she has been cheering on you guys for a while now.
- Fine, I will think about it. You two are always ganging up on me.
- Well ! Twins.
- Got it. Ray is done, we are going to watch a movie.
- Oh so cute.
- Cut it out Ariane. Goodnight you two love you both.
- We love you too and even more Ray.
- You are just like your mother.
- Goodnight bro.

I hung up and turned to find Ray dressing up just in front of me. Lucky for me he was almost done.

- Don't do that here.
- Where else, this is our room.
- Yes but it is too tempting.
- You know you are not discouraging me from doing it by saying that right?

- Yeah I just realized it after talking.
- So how was it with your siblings ?
- Ariane is excited by the news so Aiden is too. Ariane asked me to greet you and I think she is going to be bothering you even more now.
- I am used to it. I think I even like it.
- Ok good luck anyway. Let's go watch that movie.
- Hum.
- We did just that and the rest of the evening was pretty much uneventful.

<u>**Comment section :**</u>

WdoBest_84_ : I am so happy to see that the entire world knew you were acting like an idiot for most of you life

Seetrought93 : Shut it.

WdoBest_84_ : Ok but it is still true.

Sure enough my dad called the next day wondering what the hell was going on. His sentence, not mine.

What the hell is going on? Your mother has been acting weird lately, always sad and over reacting when I mention her two weeks with you. Your brother and sister telling me they don't know anything but urging me to call you. What is going on ?

- Nothing ....
- Don't tell me nothing is the matter. I want a straight answer now.
- Straight Hum ?
- What ?
- Nothing, just I would prefer to talk about it face to face.
- You did tell your siblings.
- Yes but...
- I want an answer now and no excuses.
- Dad I don't think. ...
- I am not asking you to think. I am asking you to tell me what the hell is going on. *Ray, who was listening to the conversation, sat next to me and held my hand for comfort.*

- Well dad I don't know how to tell you this but Hum....
- I am waiting.
- I am BI.
- What ? Finish your sentence. I do not understand anything.
- What I mean to say is I am bisexual.
- Oh
- Yes !
- And your mum found out how ?
- She saw me kissing Ray.
- I see. So that explains her réaction.
- Yes it does.
- Ok got it.
- Dad ?
- Yes !
- What is your reaction ?
- What do you want it to be? I don't really have any. You are my son if he is who you love I don't really have much I can do about it do I ? I am sure that is what you told her too.
- Exactly.
- So there you have it. There is not much to do. I am going to try and help her calm down before you come by home.
- Thanks dad.
- Don't worry too much she is going to come around. I really thought it was going to be something really awful. I am relieved. Goodnight son ! Good night to your friend too. I assume he is next to you.
- Yes thank you sir. Good night to you too.
- And thank you dad.
- There is no need to thank me. He then hung up.
- Well it was not that bad. Ray said.
- Yes I was not expecting that.
- What were you expecting ?
- I don't know but not that.
- Let's go to sleep I am tired tomorrow I have a lot to do at work.
- Ok. We then proceeded to lay in bed and I fell asleep in his arms.

<u>Comment section :</u>

WdoBest_84_ : Well I like your dad.

Seetrought93 : I do too. I did not picture it going exactly that way.

WdoBest_84_ : He is not religious like your mother ?

Seetrought93 : He is, my mother completely converted him.

WdoBest_84_ : Well he must have another way to see things.

Seetrought93 : I think so too and I am grateful.

WdoBest_84_ : Well I hope he can convince your mum.

Seetrought93 : Finger crossed.

The months that followed. Weeks. Long weeks that followed. She never spoke to me. We don't talk about our fights or what happened. Or anything for that matter.

In fact, when she called, she didn't ask for Ray like she used to and I understood that she needed time and that I shouldn't rush her. I knew that in some ways we'd made progress, but I couldn't see any change in her behavior except the sudden need to ignore Ray completely. And, I wasn't sure that would be enough for me. My mother was the one most affected by this.

I knew she would be the one most affected and indeed, what I realized. So I decided not to say anything. And when she asked me how I was, what was going on in my life, well, I just talked to her like before. As if she'd never known what had happened.

In fact, we did it like that again, without consulting each other again. We pretended nothing had happened. For the moment, it wasn't the right time or interest to talk on the phone about something so important anyway, so I gave her time to recover, to digest.

With all that happened since we started dating, I haven't officially had the time to move in his room yet. Even if I always slept there. So, I decided this Saturday to pack all I needed daily into his room and transforme mine into some sort of office with a bed (best type of office).

In that spirit I was sitting on the floor of my room trying to sort through my belongings, listening to loud music. Ray popped his head through the door to see how far I was in my storing process.

- I see you are not near finished !
- Nope.
- Well, do you want some help ?
- No I am in the zone I can do it by myself and am enjoying it.
- Ok. I am going to cook then, want anything in particular ?
- No surprise me.
- Got it.
- I love you.

When I heard that I dropped the book I had in my hand. I was still not completely used to our new status, and more hearing him say that on a daily basis when he never did before. Everytime I would realize the seriousness of our relationship and it would stomp me for a moment.

- You ok ? *He asked while approaching me.*
- Yeah yeah ! I am still not used to you saying that. Especially as often.
- Oh do you mind ?
- No I love it.
- Hum. *He smiled and repeated* I love you.
- I love you too, *I said, smiling back at him*
- He then left to cook us lunch while I continued with my storing process.

Comment section :

WdoBest_84_ : Oh so cute and still so boring.

Seetrought93 : Shut it, jealous.

WdoBest_84_ : I am just bored.

Seetrought93 : Yeah right.

WdoBest_84_ : You are still shy when he says he loves you ? Why is that ?

Seetrought93 : I don't know if it still seems surreal.

WdoBest_84_ : Hum !

Seetrought93 : And amazing also.

WdoBest_84_ : Ugh I am done reading mushy shit.

Seetrought93 : Yeah leave you are just bitter.

WdoBest_84_ : 😳

_ Two months later _

Finally, for the summer vacations, we spent two more weeks in Ray's apartment and mine, then went off on a romantic getaway to be free of studies. And then we both decided to go back to Bordeaux, him to his parents, me to mine. Like we usually do.

At first, my mother seemed a bit cold, she didn't talk to me much, just did what she'd done before. She didn't mention anything to me about what was going on, but she was still slightly distant. Maybe because she was afraid I'd talk about it and didn't want to. And every time I tried to have a little chat with her about, however important it was, she'd just listen, didn't want to talk to me too much, I felt like I'd lost her a bit as a confidante and Ray and I talked more and more on the phone, so she wouldn't notice (uncomfortably) all over the place. I had decided to continue my telephone therapy with Dr. Parker, and so I talked to her about how much it hurt her and Ray to feel this cold coming from my mother. Then one day.

She called and told me to take a walk with her around town to talk.

Then she told me an anecdote that surprised me. I wasn't expecting her to tell me that.She told me that one day when she was at Mass, it was the sermon that had gone wrong. I think it had something to do with Jesus talking about our neighbor, and how we should always be kind to our neighbor, and so on.

- I think it was about Jesus talking about his neighbor, how you always have to be good to your neighbor, etc. Something like that, and after mass there was a woman who was talking to her friends and she said that yes, the sermon was very interesting. But she had heard an anecdote from one of her neighbors whose son was apparently gay and she was praying hard for her son to get back on the straight and narrow because she was disgusted with the woman because her son clearly had no chance of going to heaven (his soul was damned), he was doing something so dirty and disgusting that it was a crime (sin) close to murder or that it didn't respect God's precepts. In short, she was saying something horrible and insulting. And (as if she was putting down her sweet angel like a monster, don't recognize the description.) it was on that day that she realized that in fact she had behaved as if that's what she thought of her son. That when she heard the news of my bisexuality, and my relationship with Ray, she had acted as if everything this woman said was true and that day she felt bad and ashamed. How could she have thought such a horrible and ridiculous thing about her own child? Whom she knew, whom she had raised, so gentle and kind, whose goodness she knew. And she was gradually realizing that her behavior was horrible and that this was one of the reasons why she hadn't had the courage to talk to me about how sorry she felt. She had seemed distant to me and now realized that she was continuing to hurt me and it was time for her to apologize, to ask my forgiveness for having reacted so badly. And she also wanted to have the opportunity to see Ray to apologize as well. Because just like me, she also realized that she had always suspected something but had never wanted to accept it and that she understood what I might have gone through and felt sorry for having caused it. that she had been a very bad mother and that she was going to make an effort to act better in relation to my situation and that she was going to learn to behave better and accept me as I was.

– That was all I wanted to hear from her. I burst into tears and jumped into her arms. I couldn't be happier to know that she accepts me as I am. We decided to have a little family reunion for an official announcement of sorts and everything went well and little by little her behavior with Ray improved, the prodigal son was back, she was treating him better than me again and I finally felt relieved when I saw her behavior, especially since she made it clear that she thought I couldn't make a better choice, especially when comparing him with Klaus; Because she clearly had a preference; But some time later (after some reflection) she called me back again for a little stroll (to talk while walking, to continue thinking, to hammer home the point she'd been making since childhood) She asked me with a worried look if I was still going to church. If I prayed, if I was still religious, if I still had my faith. And, I told her, don't worry, when I was 9 or ten years ago I told you that you were forcing me too much on the subject of religion and if she continued to force me so much I was just going to stop everything when I was independent and that it wasn't the kind of thing that could be forced. and that since that day we hadn't talked about it again, that she'd left me to my own devices and that I'd just go to mass because that was her only rule, and after that we'd never brought the subject up again, just that she'd noticed that I'd started praying on my own, but now, in view of the situation, she was worried. She wondered if I felt rejected by my religion. And if it was precisely because of that that I'd had doubts when I was young.

- So Mom, in fact, when I told you when I was younger that I wanted you to stop forcing me to go to church, it was just because I was too lazy to go to church.
- How? you gave me a long line about how faith is personal and if I kept forcing you without bothering to let you make your own choices, you'd just wait for the first opportunity to be out of the house and never go to church again in your life and become an atheist.
- I know exactly what I said. And it made a lot of sense. You were only nine. I don't see you making this up just to be lazy;
- Actually, I did. The first reason I said it was because you wanted me to take all the time and I was lazy. I didn't say I hadn't thought about what to say to make sure it would work.
- You had me fooled that time.
- I know. I know you too well. And besides, I didn't like formal prayers, that's all. I'm used to saying whatever I want to God in any circumstance without ever getting down on my knees first or having to make a big deal of it. It makes more sense to talk to him as if he's my best friend than to do a ton of ceremony around a formal prayer. even if sometimes I conceive I have to.
- To each his own relationship with God, I suppose.
- I agree.

We finally went home and had dinner together. It's true that she's not completely the same with Ray, but the most important thing for me is that I'm not lying to her anymore and that she's okay with everything that represents me. It's just perfect.

Comment section :

WdoBest_84_ : It's so cute.

Seetrought93 : Stop with the sarcasm.

WdoBest_84_ : No, for once I'm serious, you and your mom are adorable. Super understanding and religious and all.

Seetrought93 : Thanks? I guess.

WdoBest_84_ : You have a really low opinion of me.

Seetrought93 : It's everything you deserve.

WdoBest_84_ : Thank you so much. Since you can't see me, you should know that right now I'm crying.

Seetrought93 : Mwah. Ps I don't believe you at all.

WdoBest_84_ : As you should.

The-hot-girl_42 : Still talking too much hear !

A week later _

Yesterday I had a little get-together with my buddies. It had been over a year since we'd all seen each other. So we went to a great restaurant.

- Oh, and how was the drama?
- Not at all. Just Ray and I had a few remonstrances, if I do say so myself.
- Oh yeah? tell me about it.

So we ended up in a little Japanese restaurant that Liam had suggested and I of course came with Ray. But we were holding hands and I completely overlooked the fact that nobody knew we were going out. So we went in but holding hands all smiles and Alina saw us approaching and got up from her chair.

- I knew it. I knew it. I called it; Liam I told you, didn't I? I had every reason in the world to be jealous I knew.
- Yes, you did.
- So we're good? You two official?
- Is it? I completely forgot to warn you, I'm really sorry.

Ray, as usual, didn't say a word. Worse still, he abandoned me and went off to sit with Antoine and André. He got into an animated discussion about I don't know what manga and I stood there in front of Alina, completely confused, not knowing what to do.

- So it was really not paranoia to be jealous of Ray.
- Yeah, no, it wasn't. I'm sorry about that, I didn't realize it myself.
- Yeah.
- I'm really sorry about that.
- Mmm.
- I really am.
- Don't worry, I'm over you and I'm seeing someone.
- Cool.
- So are you all set this time?
- I think I am.
- I can see from your face that you're happy.
- Thanks, you're not bad yourself. And you Liam, what are your victims of the moment.
- I'm in a very lazy phase right now.
- I see. I think this will allow you to rest a little.
- I think so too sarcasm aside.

When we got home I sulked at Ray for abandoning me but as usual it didn't last long. IF YOU KNOW WHAT I MEAN !

Comment section :

WdoBest_84_ : Yuck again. Not interested in your honeymoon time with your boyfriend.

Seetrought93 : Yes, my boyfriend. That's super satisfying to say. My boyfriend Ray.

WdoBest_84_ : Ugh

Passeureby_102 : 🚶🚶🚶🚶🚶🚶🚶🚶🚶🚶🚶🚶🚶🚶🚶🚶🚶🚶🚶🚶🚶🚶🚶🚶

www.ingramcontent.com/pod-product-compliance
Lightning Source LLC
Chambersburg PA
CBHW081123300726
48977CB00004B/870